JOSH LACEY

HOUGHTON MIFFLIN HARCOURT
Boston New York

www.hmhco.com

The text of this book is set in Adobe Caslon.

The Library of Congress has cataloged the hardcover edition as follows:
Lacey, Josh.
The sultan's tigers / by Josh Lacey.
p. cm.
Originally published in Great Britain by Andersen Press, 2012.
Sequel to: Island of Thieves.
Summary: Tom, who comes from a long line of criminals, travels with his roguish uncle to India to find a family treasure—a bejeweled tiger stolen from the sultan's throne hundreds of years ago.
[1. Adventure and adventurers—Fiction. 2. Families—Fiction.
3. Uncles—Fiction. 4. Criminals—Fiction. 5. India—Fiction.] I. Title.
PZ7.L128Su 2013
[Fic]—dc23
2012044648
ISBN: 978-0-544-09645-5 hardcover
ISBN: 978-0-544-33629-2 paperback

Manufactured in the United States of America
DOC 10 9 8 7 6 5 4 3 2 1
4500490813

# 1

***My name is Tom Trelawney*** and I come from a long line of liars, cheats, crooks, bandits, thieves, and smugglers.

That's what my uncle says, anyway.

I'd like to believe him, but if our family consists entirely of criminals, what went wrong with my dad? He's probably the most honest person on the planet.

"He's not a real Trelawney," says Uncle Harvey. "Not like you and me."

According to my uncle, our family originally came from a small village in Cornwall, a rugged corner of England that sticks out into the Atlantic, pointing like a finger at America. The Trelawneys called themselves fishermen, but they actually made their living by piracy, smuggling illegal goods ashore and hiding them in the caves that riddle the Cornish coast.

My grandfather was a real Trelawney too.

He wasn't a pirate or a smuggler, but he never did an honest day's work in his life. He was always running from someone, always searching for a place to hide, and he left a trail of enemies all around the world.

I never really knew him.

I wish I had.

We only saw Grandpa once a year, sometimes even less. The last time he came to the States for Christmas, he drank too much wine and had a big argument with Dad.

Ten months later, he was dead.

He had a heart attack while watching TV, and that was that, kaput, he was gone.

"A good death," my mom called it, and perhaps she's right, although it's not exactly what I'd call a good death. What's wrong with being gnawed to pieces by piranhas? Or flung from a plane without a parachute? If Grandpa had died like that, I really would have been proud of him. But he died sitting in his recliner, slumped in front of the TV, according to the neighbor who found him, so maybe that really was a good death.

Grandpa had lived all over the world, but he spent the last few years of his life in a small village on the west coast of Ireland. We arrived in Shannon at dawn on the morning of the funeral. (By "we," I mean me, my mom, my dad, my little bro, Jack, and my big sister, Grace.) Dad rented a bright blue Ford Focus at the airport and drove us across the country to Grandpa's village.

Not many people came to the funeral: just us and a few neighbors.

Halfway through the service, the door squeaked open and Uncle Harvey stumbled down the aisle. "Sorry I'm late," he whispered loudly enough for everyone to hear. The vicar gave him a stern look and carried on with the sermon. Uncle Harvey grinned at us and slid into a pew on the other side of the church. I grinned back while Dad gave him a dirty look. They might be brothers, but they don't like each other much.

I was looking forward to talking to my uncle. Earlier in the year, we had traveled to Peru together, hunting down a stash of buried gold that had belonged to Sir Francis Drake. Later, back in the U.S., we'd been given dinner at the Peruvian embassy, but I hadn't seen my uncle since. I wanted to know if he'd had any more adventures. Had he been chased by crooks? Threatened by thugs? Or beat up? Had he stolen anything? Or cheated anyone? Even after spending a week with my uncle in Peru, I didn't know very much about his life, but I knew one thing for sure: it was a lot more interesting than mine.

The ceremony concluded with prayers, then we shuffled into the graveyard and stood in line to shake hands with the vicar. When my turn came, the vicar smiled down at me and said in his warm Irish accent, "So which of the grandsons are you? Are you Jack or are you Tom?"

"I'm Tom."

"Ah, the famous Tom. Your grandfather told me all about you. He said you were full of mischief. Is that true?"

"I suppose so."

"He also said he saw himself in you. I can see what he meant."

"Really?" I said. "What else did he say?"

"Oh, this and that. Maybe I'll tell you when you're a bit older." Chuckling, the vicar let go of my hand and grabbed the next in line, which happened to belong to Uncle Harvey. "Your father was a lovely man," the vicar said. "You must be missing his presence."

"I've heard him called a lot of things," said Uncle Harvey. "But never lovely. Maybe he was lovelier to you than he was to us."

The vicar looked a bit nervous, not wanting to say the wrong thing. "I didn't know your father well, but we thought of him as a valued member of the community."

"Did you really?" Uncle Harvey sounded surprised. "So he didn't steal any of your silver? Or flog your hymn books on eBay?"

"Actually, we did have a few things go missing," said the vicar. Then he noticed that my uncle was smiling. "Ah! You're having a joke with me, aren't you?"

"I'm so sorry," said Uncle Harvey. "I can't help myself."

"Even in times of trouble, it's good to have a smile on your face." The vicar beamed and moved to talk to the next person in line.

As my uncle and I walked through the churchyard, he winked at me. I winked back. Now we knew how Grandpa had been supplementing his pension.

Uncle Harvey said, "How's life, kid?"

"It's OK. A little boring. How's yours?"

"I would say it's good, but my dad's just died so I probably shouldn't. How often did you see the old man?"

"Not very often," I replied. "He sometimes visited us for Christmas. But he and Dad always ended up arguing."

"He argued with everyone. That was just his way."

"Did you argue with him too?"

"All the time," said Uncle Harvey. "But we always made up again. He was like that. We'd get drunk together and have a big row, then forget all about it the next day. It's a pity you won't get to know him better. Did you ever come and stay with him?"

"Dad wouldn't let me. I don't know why not."

"I do," said Uncle Harvey.

"Yeah? Why?"

"He knows that as far as he's concerned, the Trelawney genes skipped a generation. You're more like your grandfather than your father. He must have been worried about what would happen if the two of you ever got together. Just like he's worried about the two of us. And he's right, isn't he? Ah, hello, Simon. How are you?"

Simon is my dad. He didn't look particularly pleased to see his brother, but maybe he was just feeling sad. I guess you would feel sad if your father died, even if the two of you had furious arguments whenever you happened to be in the same room at the same time.

The brothers shook hands. Then Uncle Harvey kissed my mom on both cheeks and said hello to Jack and Grace.

"I've invited the vicar to join us for lunch," my father said to Harvey. "Can you give him a lift in your car? There isn't much room in ours."

"Sure. Where are we going?"

"I've booked a table at a restaurant on the coast. Apparently it's very good. You can follow me there."

"Great. I'll go and get the vicar."

Once Uncle Harvey was striding across the churchyard, Dad turned to me. "Here are the keys to Grandpa's house. We'll see you there in a couple of hours."

I took the keys and stared stupidly at my father. "Why are you giving me these?"

"Because you're going to go to the house."

"What am I supposed to do there?"

"Whatever you like. Read a book, play a game. It's up to you."

"What about lunch?"

"What *about* lunch?"

"Why can't I come to lunch?"

"You know why not."

"Because I'm grounded?"

"Exactly."

"But this is Grandpa's funeral! You've got to let me come to the lunch!"

"I'm afraid not, Tom. You're grounded."

"That's so unfair!"

"You should have thought about that before you stole the golf cart. We'll be a couple of hours. See you later."

"Dad—"

"Don't 'Dad' me."

"But, Dad—"

"I said don't 'Dad' me."

"But, Dad, it's just not fair."

"See you later," said my father, showing not a trace of sympathy. "Go on. Go to the house."

Grace tried to argue on my behalf, which was nice of her, and Jack said he wouldn't mind staying with me, which was nice of him, too, but Dad asked if they both wanted to be grounded as well, and of course they didn't. He told them to go to the car. Grace grinned at me and Jack gave me a thumbs-up, then they sloped away. Dad turned back to me. "I'm sorry, Tom. I don't like doing this. I wish there were some other way. But you've really given me no choice."

I looked at my dad for a moment. Then I said, "You're an idiot."

His face turned red and he told me never to talk to him like that, and Mom said I should remember where I was, but I didn't care. I turned my back on my parents and walked away, their angry voices following me out of the graveyard.

# 2

**I'd been grounded** for a month. It was my own stupid fault. I had been caught borrowing a golf cart from the local golf course. The groundskeepers said I was stealing. I said I wasn't stealing, I was borrowing. They said what's the difference? I said the difference is that I would have brought it back again. They said how do we know you would have brought it back? I said you have to trust me. They said how can we trust you when you steal things? I said I wasn't stealing, I was borrowing, but by that time no one was listening.

It was so unfair. Of course I wasn't stealing their golf cart. I just wanted to have a bit of fun and drive around the course. Unfortunately I'd only gotten as far as the first hole when two groundskeepers came running after me.

I gunned the throttle and tried to lose them, and probably would have if some idiot hadn't planted a tree right where I wanted to go.

Which was how I now came to find myself walking down the street to Grandpa's house while the rest of my family drove twelve miles to the nearest nice restaurant.

I wanted to be there. I wanted my lunch. I wanted to see Uncle Harvey. And more than anything, I wanted to hear about all the crazy things that Grandpa had done in his long and disreputable existence.

Yeah, I know, I shouldn't have stolen that golf cart.

Even better, I shouldn't have gotten caught.

But I couldn't help myself. I'm a Trelawney. We do dumb things like stealing golf carts.

As I walked down the street, I thought about Grandpa and wondered how he ended up living here, a wet village on the western coast of nowhere. What did he do all day? This village seemed nice enough, but it wasn't exactly exciting. I wouldn't have chosen to live here. Or die here.

All the other houses had mowed lawns and beds of bright flowers, but Grandpa's looked as if no one had lived there for years. Paint was peeling off the front door. There was a hole in one of the windows. The front garden was a jumble of weeds and brambles, plus the odd broken bottle and what looked like the remains of a bicycle. Because I'd been here before, I knew Grandpa's house hadn't been wrecked in the days since his death; it had always looked like this. He didn't bother with fixing it up. Or even cleaning.

Inside, things were even worse. The house was a danger zone. The kitchen sink was blocked and the stove was caked with dried food. In the hallway, the light switch had fallen off. Exposed wires drooled out of the wall. It was a miracle Grandpa had survived so long.

I went hunting for food. The fridge contained nothing

but some carrots covered in black spots and a half-drunk carton of milk with a sell-by date of three weeks ago, but I found some cans of tomato soup in a cupboard. I opened one and tipped the contents into a saucepan. When the soup was piping hot, I poured it into a bowl and ate my lunch in front of the TV, flicking through every channel. There was nothing on. I feel sorry for the Irish. Their TV is lame.

Grandpa had a few books and there were some old magazines lying around, but I didn't feel like reading. So I explored the house, looking through the rooms, poking around, seeing what I could find. I don't know what I was looking for, but I hoped I might uncover some curious treasure from one of Grandpa's adventures.

I was standing in his bedroom, staring at the suits and shirts hanging in his wardrobe, when I heard a sound like breaking glass. It seemed to have come from downstairs.

I stood very still, listening.

Had I imagined it?

Yes, I must have imagined it.

Then I heard the noise again. Another smash. More glass tinkling. As if someone was knocking the loose pieces out of a windowpane.

Why would anyone want to break into this house?

Maybe it wasn't a person. Maybe it was a cat hunting for a warm place to take a nap.

I decided to investigate.

I took three steps along the landing and heard a loud thump.

That wasn't a cat. That was the sound of feet slamming down on the floor. Now I could hear them crunching on the glass that they'd just knocked out of the window.

I could have run. I could have hidden. I could have snuck into the wardrobe in Grandpa's bedroom or jumped out of an upstairs window. But it was daylight and I was in my own grandfather's house, so I thought I'd be able to look after myself.

Anyway, I knew what I'd find when I went downstairs.

A kid like me.

Who else would break into an empty house?

I've done it myself. If you're bored on a Saturday afternoon and the town is quiet and your friends are otherwise occupied, what could be better than sneaking into a derelict house and poking around? I like seeing what's left behind. Sometimes people have to get out in a hurry and they discard everything—all the junk they couldn't carry, clothes and TVs and tins of tuna fish. Once I found a twenty-dollar bill in the crack of a kitchen drawer. Another time, I found a white bag stuffed with plastic giraffes. Who could possibly want a hundred plastic giraffes? I took one as a memento. It's still on a shelf in my bedroom.

Anyway, that's how I knew who would have broken into Grandpa's house. It would just be someone looking for a bit of excitement. Some kid who lived in this boring little village on the edge of nowhere and wanted to get a kick from exploring some dead guy's abandoned home. If I was really lucky, he might want to hang out with me for the next couple of hours while I was waiting for my family to come back from lunch.

I jogged down the stairs and headed along the hallway. I was just about to stroll into the sitting room and make some quip, looking forward to startling the kid who'd dared to break into my grandad's house, when a man appeared out of the shadows.

"Not another step," he said, his voice low and threatening.

"Who are you?" I stammered. "What are you—?"

He swung at me. I dodged backwards, but he managed to grab me around the neck. I held his arm with both hands. His fingers pressed into my throat. I struggled. Lurched backwards. Tried to wriggle out of his grasp. Then I felt something pressing into my side and knew it was a knife. He'd just have to push a bit harder and the blade would be sliding between my ribs. I went very still.

He was a big guy. Much taller than me. Much broader, too. His eyes were dark and cold. "Who's here?" he hissed. "Who else?"

"No one," I said, then cursed myself for telling the truth. Why didn't I say my friend the black belt was coming over for lunch?

"When will they be back?"

"Who?"

He pressed the knife deeper into my side. "When will they be back?"

"Soon."

"How soon?"

It's difficult to think straight when you've got a knife pushing against your ribs, and so, like an idiot, I told him exactly what he wanted to know. I guess I was nervous. I even told him the restaurant was twelve miles away, whereas if I'd been thinking straight, I would have said it was just around the corner and my folks might be back any minute. I probably would have told him about being grounded and the unfairness of it all, but he interrupted me: "What's your name?"

"Tom."

"This way, Tom. And keep quiet. If you make a noise, I'm gonna hurt you. Got that?"

"Yes."

"You sure?"

"Yes."

"Come on, then."

He half pushed, half dragged me down the hallway and in to the kitchen.

I knew who he was. I'd heard about this. There are thieves who read the local papers, looking for announcements of weddings and funerals, the days that houses will definitely be empty. He must be one of them. Well, he was wasting his time today. There was nothing worth stealing in Grandpa's house. Not unless you wanted eleven cans of tomato soup or some very smelly socks.

The only thing was, this guy didn't look like a crook. Not

the type of crook who breaks into empty houses, anyway. His clothes were too nice.

If I'd seen him in the street or been shown a photo of him, I would have guessed he was a soldier or an athlete. Maybe a tennis player. He was a big guy with broad shoulders and strong hands. He had a long face, a strong chin, and a great tan. He had to live somewhere sunny. So he wasn't from around here.

He didn't sound local, either. I couldn't place his accent, but I was almost sure he wasn't Irish. His words had more of a twang. He might have been South African or Australian, something like that.

Once we were through the door, he told me to turn around. For a terrible moment I thought he was going to slit my throat. Instead he slipped a dishcloth into my mouth and tied it tight.

I tried to scream, but I didn't have enough breath in my lungs, and before I could suck in any more, he was tipping me forward and yanking my hands behind my back. He was too strong for me. I couldn't wriggle away. I heard him opening a kitchen drawer. Slamming it. Opening another. He must have found what he was looking for, because he started working quickly and efficiently, tying my hands behind my back with what felt like a piece of string, then sitting me down in a chair and strapping me to that.

He put his face close to mine.

"I don't want to hurt you," he said. "But if you make a noise or try to get away, I *will* kill you."

# 3

**I don't get scared easily,** but this guy filled me with fear. I don't know what it was. His eyes, maybe, or his voice, or simply the way he'd crept up on me and grabbed me from out of nowhere. Whatever it was, I knew I didn't want to mess with him. He was serious about killing me, I could hear that in his voice. I sat very still, listening to him pacing around the house. Was he a thief? If so, why had he bothered breaking in to this house? And wouldn't he leave as soon as he saw the way Grandpa had lived? The TV must have been a hundred years old and nothing else in the house was worth anything. What could this guy possibly be looking for?

I heard him moving through the ground floor, room by room, then heading up the stairs. His footsteps were directly above me. This was my chance. I didn't want to stick around and allow him to kill me. Even if he heard me, he'd take a few seconds to come all the way downstairs. That should be enough time to get out of here.

I started wriggling my arms. My phone was in my pocket. If only I could stretch a little further . . .

No. Impossible. The string was tied so tightly, I could hardly move.

I shuffled from side to side. Pulled my arms up and pushed them down again. Shrugged my shoulders. Twisted my wrists. Strained every muscle.

Finally I got frustrated and started jerking my arms halfway out of their sockets, ignoring how much it hurt, just trying to get free. The chair's legs suddenly lifted off the ground. I tipped forward and landed face-first, smacking my forehead into Grandpa's floor. For a moment I was stunned. *No problem*, I thought to myself. *I'll crawl out of here. Take the chair with me.* I scrabbled across the floor like a wounded crab, heading for the door.

I heard his laughter before I saw him. "What are you doing? You think I don't know how to tie a knot? Come on, kid. Let me help you." He must have heard me clattering around and come back to the kitchen. He bent down, reached out a hand, and yanked off my gag. I was still gasping for breath when he picked up the chair, swung it around, and plonked me down as if I weighed nothing at all. We were face-to-face, me sitting and him bent double, peering into my face. "You all right?"

"I won't tell anyone you're here," I begged. He sounded sympathetic, but I didn't believe a word of it. He'd just threatened to kill me; why should he suddenly be worrying if I was all right? "Please, just let me go."

"I will. In a minute. First we need to talk. What's your name again?"

"Tom."

"That's right. Now, Tom, I need you to help me. Your gramps and me, we were doing a deal together. He's broken his side of the bargain by dying, but I want to keep mine. I'm looking for something. It's in this house, but I don't know where. You're going to help me find it."

"What is it?" I asked.

"Just some old papers. Nothing interesting."

He reached into his belt and pulled out his knife. Before I could even think about screaming, he was slitting the string that bound my wrists.

"You can get up if you want," he said. "But don't bother trying to run away."

I stood and flexed my wrist, getting the blood moving into my veins. Why was he being so friendly? Was it a trick? I glanced at the door. Should I make a run for it? I looked back at him and I could see he knew what I was thinking, but he wasn't worried. He knew I wouldn't get three paces before he tripped me up, knocked me down, and stuck a knife in my ribs.

"I'm Marko," he said.

"Mark-oh?"

"That's right."

"Nice to meet you, Marko. Not."

He grinned. "You're like the old man, aren't you?"

"You knew him?"

"We were good friends."

"Yeah, right."

"Maybe not exactly friends. You can call us colleagues if you'd rather. We were working together. He had something I wanted. I was going to buy it off him. Now he's gone and I can't find it. Where is it, Tom? Where would the old guy hide something he wanted to keep hidden?"

"I don't know."

"You can do better than that."

"I really don't."

"Do I have to tie you up again?"

"No. But I don't know where your stuff is."

Marko looked at me for a moment as if he was trying to decide whether I could be trusted. Then he said, "Do you want to earn five hundred euros?"

"Sure."

"I'm looking for a bundle of old papers. I want them, Tom, and I'm willing to pay for them. Help me find these papers and I'll give you five hundred euros."

"No, you won't."

"What do you mean?"

"If I find the papers, you'll just steal them."

"You're wrong, Tom. I'm an honest guy. If I make a deal, I keep it. Here's the money." He took out his thick wallet and counted five notes. He offered them to me. I reached for the money, but he pulled it away immediately. "Find the papers first," he said.

Five hundred euros. That was more than six hundred dollars. Enough to buy a new computer or a new bike.

I didn't like Marko. And I certainly didn't trust him. But I could deal with five hundred euros.

"What's in these papers?" I said.

"They're just some documents."

"What sort of documents?"

"Historical ones."

"Why do you want them?"

"I'm working for a collector," said Marko. "He loves all this old stuff. He wants it for his collection."

"How much is he paying for them?"

"That's my business, Tom."

"How much were you going to pay my grandfather?"

"A decent amount."

"More than five hundred euros?"

"A bit more."

"How much more?"

"Like I said, a bit more."

"I'm not going to help you unless you tell me."

"If you really want to know, we agreed on two thousand euros. It's a fair price. Your grandfather got in touch with my boss and said he had something to sell. How were we meant to know if he was telling the truth? So I came over here to have a chat with him and see what he was selling. We had a nice chat. I went back to talk to my boss. Next thing I heard, your grandpa was dead."

"So you thought you'd break in to the house and steal these documents instead?"

"That's right," said Marko, smiling as if he had nothing to be ashamed of. "But I can't find them. You know this house better than I do. What do you say? Will you help me?"

"I don't see why not," I said. "For two thousand euros."

"That's not the deal, mate. We said five hundred."

"Two thousand or nothing."

He laughed. "You really are just like the old man, aren't you?"

"He was my grandfather."

"I guess he was. Let's say a thousand."

"Two." I smiled, trying to look a lot braver (and more relaxed) than I actually felt. I remembered how Uncle Harvey dealt with negotiations. He just smiled and pretended he didn't care. So that's what I tried to do too.

It must have worked, because Marko raised his price. "I'll give you fifteen hundred."

"Two thousand euros or nothing."

Marko thought for a moment. Then he nodded. "Fine. You got me. It's a deal. Where are they?"

"I don't know."

"I thought you said . . . You little creep." His hand reached for the knife.

"Wait." I backed away, my arms up. "I'll find them."

"You just said you don't know where they are."

"I don't. But I'll find them."

"How?"

"I'll search this house."

"I don't believe this."

His lip curled and I suddenly thought I'd made a terrible mistake, trying to play him. I backtracked as fast as I could. "You don't have to worry. I'm going to find them. I will. I promise."

"You'd better."

"I said I will."

"Come on, then. Where are they?"

"Give me a minute. Let me think."

"We don't have time for thinking. Just find them."

I glanced at the knife, then Marko's face. If I actually gave him these documents, would he really pay me two thousand euros? Or would he grab what he wanted and stab me?

I didn't want to think about that now.

I just smiled and said, "Let's go this way."

I remembered my grandfather. I thought about my uncle. I told myself: *This is the way to be a real Trelawney. I don't want to be the type of person who surrenders to fear. I'm not going to give up. I'm a Trelawney!* Sure, I was scared. Of course I was. This guy was probably planning to kill me. I just had to keep him talking, make him think I was going to give him the documents, and hope my folks hadn't ordered another bottle of wine to toast Grandpa's memory.

We did the living room first, then the kitchen and the downstairs bathroom. Marko must have been through all that already, but he just stood back and watched me search again, opening drawers and cupboards, lifting carpets, tapping floorboards, hunting for hiding places. I could sense his eyes on me all the time.

We went upstairs to Grandpa's bedroom. Under the bed, I encountered three socks, a beer bottle, and an apple core so ancient that it crumbled into dust as I tried to pick it up, but no historical documents, nothing that could possibly be worth two thousand euros.

There were two more rooms on that floor and an attic above, accessed by a shaky metal ladder. We went through everything, even pulling up loose floorboards and checking the water tank.

We were walking downstairs again, heading for the garden and its mossy old shed, when I finally heard the noise that I'd been waiting for: a car pulling up outside. Marko hurried to the window. A second car was parking behind the first.

Marko glanced at me.

For a moment I thought he was going to pull out the knife and shut me up permanently. Or would he kidnap me, force me to go with him? Instead he said, "I need those letters, Tom. You'd better find them. I'll be watching you."

Then he was gone, running down the stairs and leaving the house through the back door.

# 4

**A moment later there was** a knock at the door. I opened it. My brother and sister were standing there, looking smug and well fed.

"Hi, bro," said Jack.

"Hi."

"We brought you a doggy bag." Grace held up something wrapped in silver foil. "We thought you must be hungry."

"I've had lunch, thanks."

"What did you have?"

"I found a can of soup."

"Was it delicious?"

"It was OK."

"Ours was delicious. I had smoked salmon, followed by lamb noisettes on a bed of creamed spinach, and a chocolate pudding for dessert." Grace takes notes whenever she eats out. She wants to be a celebrity chef when she grows up.

"I had steak and fries," said my little brother.

*I got mugged by a guy with a knife,* I could have said. Instead, I thanked my sister for the doggy bag and scooted into the house before Mom and Dad arrived. I was surprised they hadn't commented on my appearance. Didn't I look like a guy who'd just been tied up, knocked over, and pushed around? Obviously I didn't. I must have looked like just my normal self.

Once I was safely inside the living room, I stood for a moment with my back against the door, waiting for my parents to come and bug me, but they must have decided to leave me alone. That was lucky. I needed some time to myself. I had to check out these historical documents, whatever they were. I wanted to know why they were worth two thousand euros.

As soon as Marko started talking about them, I knew where they would be hidden.

While he was interrogating me, I had tried to push the knowledge out of my mind, not wanting to give any sign that I'd solved his mystery for him.

We didn't visit Grandpa often. He lived three thousand miles away, but that wasn't why. We wouldn't have visited much even if he'd lived next door. He and Dad couldn't spend more than a few minutes in the same room without arguing. But we once came to Ireland on vacation and stopped for lunch in Grandpa's house. Mom, Dad, Grace, and Jack went for a walk in the afternoon, leaving me with Grandpa. He talked to me, telling me some stuff about his life and giving me several pieces of advice, which I'm sure were very useful, although unfortunately I can't remember a single thing he said. But one thing did lodge in my mind. He had shown me something that he called his treasure box.

Shelves filled the niches on either side of the fireplace. Most of them were crammed with all kinds of junk—old magazines, tangled wires, jam jars filled with nails, a stack of crappy DVDs—but two of the shelves were filled with books. I scanned the spines, running my eyes over the titles and the names of the authors. None of them meant anything to me. None of the books looked familiar. Had it gone? Had he moved it? Or was it there and I just couldn't remember what it was called?

Then I saw what I was looking for. A thick hardback, the creased leather spine embossed with faded gold letters:

> Cornish Highways and Byways; a Description of Some Rambles Around Penzance, Land's End and Zennor, Incorporating Illustrations of Local Personalities and Wildlife by Edward Charles Trelawney

I pulled the book from its shelf and opened the front cover. The pages had been cut away, leaving a gap, a space, a place to keep valuables.

The day that I was last here, my grandfather had pointed it out on the shelf. He said, "Do you want to see a book written by one of your ancestors?"

When I pulled it down and opened it up, he started laughing. "You didn't really think a Trelawney had written a book, did you? Most of us can't even read."

This was his secret hiding place. Then it had contained a wad of twenty-pound notes and a chunky gold necklace.

Now it was full of letters.

Two thousand euros' worth of old letters scrawled in faded ink on crinkly paper.

Was Marko really going to be watching me?

He said he would and there was no reason to doubt him. He might be parked across the street. I just had to walk out of the front door holding the letters. He couldn't steal them from me in broad daylight. He'd have to make a deal. *Give me the money. Give me the two thousand you agreed on with Grandpa.*

I didn't want to hand them over right away. I wanted to know what they really were, and why they were worth so much to Marko.

I opened the door. I could hear voices from the kitchen and the clatter of cutlery and dishes. The rest of my family had gotten to work. They were tidying the house. We had to make it respectable before the real estate agents arrived on Monday morning, the day after tomorrow.

Hoping no one would hear me and tell me to come and help, I snuck upstairs to Grandpa's bedroom. His bed was saggy and damp—the sheets probably hadn't been changed all year—but it was comfy enough, so I sat with my back against the headboard, picked the first letter from the top of the pile, and started reading.

*7 June 1795, Southampton, Hants.*

*Dear Miss Pickering,*

*I much enjoyed our conversation at last night's ball and hope I may have the pleasure of conversing with you again at your soonest convenience. Our departure has been delayed once more, so with your permission, and that of your mama, would you care to visit the fair with me this coming Saturday? There is supposedly a man with two heads, and a rhinocepede from deepest Africa. If you would agree to accompany me, I should be the happiest man in England.*

*Your devoted servant,*

*Horatio Trelawney*

That made sense. Now I knew why the letters were here. Horatio Trelawney must have been one of us. The letters were a family heirloom. Had they been passed down from generation to generation until they reached Grandpa? Why didn't anyone else know about them? And why did Marko? I didn't understand why a bunch of old letters would be worth anything to a guy like him. There must some information in them. Unless Grandpa had conned him, of course. I'd already seen how Uncle Harvey cheated money out of rich men, playing on their vanity. He'd sold a Picasso to Otto Gonzalez in Peru for a hundred thousand dollars, an amazing price for a painting that should have been worth six or seven million, and Otto had been delighted with his purchase until he discovered it was actually a worthless fake. Like father, like son. Maybe Grandpa had done the same thing. Maybe he'd written these letters himself, faking the ink and the paper to make them look old. But why would he do that? Who would he have been trying to cheat? Historians? Collectors? Why should they want these letters? Why should they care about Horatio Trelawney's love life?

Questions, questions, questions, but no answers yet.

*Patience,* I told myself. There were a lot more letters to read. A whole box packed with them. Maybe the secret was hidden further down the stack.

I put the first letter face-down on the bed, picked up the next one, and opened the crinkly paper on my knees.

*19 June 1795, Southampton, Hants.*

*My dear Miss Pickering,*

*Thank you for your letter of Friday last. Of course your mother and both your sisters would be more than welcome to join us. I should not like to visit the theatre unchaperoned! Lord knows what the good people of Southampton might think. I shall call for you at your house at six o'clock on Tuesday next. Thank you for the gift of Clarissa, which looks like a very fine book, although I have not yet had a chance to read beyond the first page. Our battalion has been excessive busy with parades.*

*With fondest wishes,*

*Your newest friend,*

*Horatio Trelawney*

Maybe Marko had been telling the truth. Maybe he wasn't lying to me or trying to cheat me. He hadn't fought with Grandpa or killed him. These letters might really be nothing more than historical documents, describing the dreary life of one of my ancestors.

Then why would Marko want them? Why would he break into a house and tie me up, just for a bunch of crinkly old love letters?

I unfolded the next letter.

*18 August 1795, near Dublin, Ireland.*

*My dearest Miss Pickering,*

*We have been in this bog-ridden, rain-sodden country for a fortnight now. The food is foul-tasting. The natives are foul-tempered. I would give my right arm to be back in Southampton. No, I would not give my right arm, nor my left neither, for I would need both of them to hold my sweet Susan. I enclose a small token of my affections. Please write to me at the barracks here in Dublin. The address is on this envelope. I hope to see you within two months at the very most.*

*With all affection,*

*Your devoted admirer,*

*Horatio Trelawney*

A voice shouted up the stairs. "Tom!"

It was Mom. She'd probably seen the broken window and wanted to blame it on me.

I shouted back: "Yes!"

"Where are you?"

"In Grandpa's room."

"What are you doing up there?"

"Nothing."

"Can you come down here, please?"

"Why?"

"Just come down here, please!"

I snuck the letters under the duvet and headed out, trying to think of an excuse to explain the smashed window and the broken glass on the floor.

She and Dad were standing at the bottom of the stairs. He was struggling with a vacuum cleaner and she had her arms folded.

"The rest of us are cleaning up the house," said Mom. "Would you like to help?"

Ah, that was good. They must have thought the window had been broken before. Grandpa must have done it himself, they'd decided, or a bird or a fox had bashed it out while the house was empty. Well, I couldn't see any reason why I should help them clean up the house. Not after the way they'd treated me. So I shook my head. "No."

"Tom—"

"I said no."

"Tom—"

"You wouldn't take me to Grandpa's funeral lunch."

"Yes, but—"

"So I don't see why I should help clean up the house."

"Tom, it's not—"

"I'm going back upstairs."

"Tom. Come back here, Tom! *Tom!*"

I was already halfway up the stairs. She could have run after me. She could have threatened me with all kinds of unusual punishments. She could have done just about anything, but she didn't, because, I think, she knew I was right and she was wrong. They really should have taken me to the lunch.

# 5

*12 September 1798. Aboard the Audacious. Somewhere in the middle of the ocean, although I know not where, nor do I much care.*

*My dear Susanna,*

*Life aboard a ship is exceeding monotonous, particularly when you are a soldier and a landlubber, and have no job, no task, nothing to occupy your hands or your mind. I have taken to walking the decks for hours each day, excepting when the storms have hit us, and then I have huddled below decks in the company of my fellow officers, cursing the demons who enrage the skies, spitting us with rain and hurling us about with waves as big as a house.*

*We have been a week without sight of land. Yesterday a whale swam alongside us. We fired muskets at him but he appeared not even to notice them.*

*In the wind, the ship shrieks like a pig running from the butcher. I hope she will not fall apart. A man could not survive longer than a few minutes in these waters.*

*I wish now I had taken my father's suggestion and*

*returned to my native Cornwall. I think often and fondly of the farm that awaits us, the fields to be tilled. If only we had the money to buy it! Let me make my fortune once we arrive in India, my dearest wife, and bring it home, and then we shall purchase the house that we deserve.*

*I do not know when I shall have a chance to send this letter to you, nor when it might arrive in Southampton, but I must write to you nevertheless, missing you so fervently as I am. I shall add this letter to the pile that I have wrote and send them when we reach dry land.*

*How is little Thomas? And my darling Charlotte? Give them each a kiss from their father. I miss them more than I can say. I only hope I shall survive these rolling seas and dark skies and return to see them soon.*

*With all warm affection from your seasick husband,*

*Horatio*

That wasn't very exciting. Horatio sounded more like my dad than Grandpa or Uncle Harvey. Maybe the Trelawney genes had skipped him, too.

I added that letter to the pile on the bed and unfolded the next one, in which Horatio arrived in India. He complained about the heat, the bugs, the food, his fellow officers, and the men under his command.

What did I know about India? Not much. I could find it on a map. I knew the main religion was Hinduism and the women wore dresses called saris. I'm pretty good friends with an Indian kid at school, Kartick, and I've been to his house a few times, but it wasn't much different from anyone else's. You wouldn't even know he was Indian. He was born in the States and I think his mom and dad were too.

Curry. That was the one Indian thing that I knew about. I'd eaten enough of it. Rogan josh is my favorite. Lamb, not chicken. That's pretty much my favorite meal. A couple of crackly poppadoms to start with, please, then a plate of lamb rogan josh with pilau rice and some naan bread.

All this thought of curry was making me hungry. I opened the doggy bag that Grace had given me, nibbled the contents—I wasn't quite sure what they were, but they tasted great—and kept on reading. The next few letters described the dreary routines of a soldier stationed in a foreign country without much to do. Horatio's days were taken up with parades and inspections. He had to check that every soldier under his command was carrying a clean musket and a supply of powder. He developed a red rash on his legs and spent three weeks in bed with an upset stomach. He wrote a whole letter about his wife's homemade plum pudding and how he would have given a year's salary just to taste it. Then he went back to complaining about the heat, the food, the boredom, and the prickly rash, which had spread up his back and onto his arms.

In the next letter, things got a bit more exciting.

*13 January 1799, Madras.*

*My dear Susanna,*

*We have our orders! The army is marching today. Our*

*final destination is supposedly a secret, although everyone knows where we are going, even the men. West to Mysore. To fight the man that they call the Tiger. His real name is Tippoo Sultan. I have heard stories of him, but I shall not scare you with them. He is said to be rich. If we fight him and win, the booty will be magnificent. I shall come home laden with diamonds! I must hurry, we are called. I must speed to deliver this before we march.*

*I am, as always,*
*your adoring husband,*
*Horatio*

*Diamonds,* I thought.

Maybe Horatio found them. Maybe he hid them. Maybe Grandpa had got them. Maybe . . .

I unfolded the next letter from the pile.

# 6

*28 April 1799, Seringapatam.*

*My dearest Susanna,*

*The siege has begun in earnest. Every day, the guns blast from dawn till dusk. The noise is almost unbelievable. I have taken to plugging my ears with cotton. Smoke hangs over the landscape. Men scurry through the lines, carrying weapons and orders. We are in a frenzy of anticipation, awaiting the command to advance.*

*I am afeared of dying, not so much for myself as for you and the little uns. Almost as much, I am afeared of killing. I hinted so much to the trusty Sergeant Entwhistle and he advised me not to worry. He said, should I find myself confronted by a ferocious Hindoo, I should know what to do soon enough, and would do it too. Given the choice between living and dying, something within us briskly makes the decision, and we forget all our discomfort at the idea of killing another member of our own species. So he said, having seen many battles, and I am sure he is quite correct.*

*I do not know where I should be without Sergeant Entwhistle. Adrift, certainly. Most probably dead already. Should I lose my footing, or my composure, or should my courage desert me in the face of death, he will rule the men on my behalf.*

*I saw a man die yesterday.*

*The Hindoos have a strange contraption which they aim at us, a long-barrelled weapon which fires explosive rockets. They shoot through the air, screeching like angry cats. Usually we have the time to move ourselves aside before they land in our midst, but young Ruddles was too absorbed by his breakfast, and did not even hear us shouting at him to move himself.*

*He was a sweet-faced boy, just a week past his fifteenth birthday, and he was eating a crust of bread when the rocket descended from the sky and broke his skull in half. We buried him last night.*

*Baird and Wellesley have been walking through the lines, inspecting the men and querying the officers. Neither knows my name, but I have spoken with them both.*

*Baird is a bad-tempered Scotsman who was captured by Tippoo in a previous engagement some years since, and spent two years in the city's dungeons, where he is said to have been chained to the wall and forced to stand neck-deep in water for month after month. You can imagine his passion for revenge.*

*Wellesley is quite different, a lean-faced man with a long nose and a cruel mouth. His brother Richard is the*

*Governor-General in Calcutta and the men whisper that Wellesley owes his advancement to this fact alone. I am not sure that I agree with them. His manner suggests a real soldier and inspires respect. If I was to follow anyone through the smoke of battle, I would be happy enough to follow him.*

*Soon the bombardment will cease, the smoke will clear, and the order will be heard along the lines. I shall seal this letter now and write again on the other side of the battle.*

*Horatio*

The door opened. Grace stepped into the room. She said, "What are you doing?"

"Nothing."

She pointed at the letter in my hand. "What's that?"

"Nothing."

"What is it?"

"Sorry, Grace. It's a secret. I can't tell you any more. Do you mind me leaving me alone?"

"I can't."

"Why not?"

"Mom told me to clean in here."

"You can do it later. I'm in here now."

"But Mom said—"

"I don't care what Mom said."

Grace looked at me for a moment. Then she said, "Are you OK?"

"I'm fine."

"Sure?"

"Sure."

"OK. See you later."

She closed the door behind her. A moment later, I heard the sound of the vacuum cleaner starting up in the corridor. I went back to the letters. I'd almost reached the end. There were only three or four more pieces of paper left in the hollowed-out book.

*5 May 1799, Seringapatam.*

*My dearest Susanna,*

*The battle is over. A pall of smoke hangs over the city. Blood flows through the streets. Screams echo in the night. Our men have gone wild. Nothing restrains them, nothing holds them back. They have been killing and thieving as if the world will be ended before dawn, as if tomorrow will never come, as if all goodness and rightness has ebbed out of their blood.*

*My dear wife, I have seen sights that you could not imagine. I only hope I can forget them.*

*At four o'clock this afternoon, Baird led two hundred men to the walls. They scaled the barricades and overcame the line and raced along the battlements. The town was taken almost there and then. Seeing their success, our men flooded forward.*

*Fighting continued through the streets till dusk and*

*beyond. I led a small troop toward the palace. We met some fierce resistance, but lost only one of our party, my faithful Sergeant Entwhistle. He took a dagger in his gut. I shall never forget the expression on his face as he sat down, holding the knife's handle in his own hand, and stared at the blood pouring from his belly. So surprised he looked, as if he could not imagine how such a thing could have come to pass. Then his eyes rolled and he was gone.*

*I left a man to guard his body, so he should not be assaulted by the natives while he lay there, and we fought onwards, resolving to return and give dear old Entwhistle a true Christian burial when the battle was entirely won.*

*We moved swiftly through the streets, fighting hand to hand, bayonet to body. Soon we came to the palace. Tippoo himself was nowhere to be seen. We whipped quickly through the palace. The enemy ran from us. We dispatched any who remained.*

*The palace itself was a scene of wonder. My powers of description are so weak, I cannot paint it adequately in words. I can simply say that I have seen nothing comparable, not even in the finest houses in England.*

*We met some men from the 15th, who told us Tippoo was dead. They had seen his corpse themselves, sprawled in the dust on the battlements. They are saying that he was killed by a British soldier, who shot him through the forehead and stole the jewels hanging about his neck. The name of this soldier is not known. He has not come forward. If*

*Wellesley wishes to find him, he will have to search the baggage of every man in the army.*

*I am being called. I shall write more later.*

. . .

*A day has passed. I am continuing this letter on my bed. I have a small wound on my leg. You need not worry, my dearest wife. It is nothing more than a scratch, the cut from a Hindoo's sabre. He caught me with his blade before I could dispatch him.*

*The surgeon tells me that the sores should heal in a week or two. He has not time to dress the wound yet, because his attention is devoted to more serious cases, those who have lost an arm or a leg.*

*The city is quiet. Wellesley allowed the rampage to continue for a day and night, but now he has imposed a curfew and forbidden any more theft or destruction. The men are not happy. Some cannot hold themselves back. Four of our soldiers are to be hanged for looting. Another thirty have been flogged. But they were only the ones who had the misfortune to be caught, the others have escaped scot free with their loot.*

*Tippoo Sultan's treasures have vanished into the pockets of our army. His gold, his diamonds, all are gone. So is the necklace said to be made from pearls the size of hens' eggs. And so too are the tigers which stood on his throne, each of them speckled with rubies and emeralds. Wellesley has issued an order: he wishes Tippoo's own treasures for*

*England and King George. Whoever has them will be keeping them well hidden.*

*With all adoration,*
*And in haste,*
*Your beloved husband,*
*Horatio*

# 7

**I liked the sound** of the gold. And the necklace of pearls as big as eggs. Was this why Marko was so desperate to get his hands on these "historical documents"? Had Horatio stolen some of these treasures himself? Or given a clue to where they could be found? Or was Marko really just interested in these letters as historical artifacts? There were only a few sheets of paper left in the box. I must be close to the heart of the mystery. I pulled out the next letter.

*13 or 14 May 1799, I am not sure of the precise day, Seringapatam.*

*My darling wife,*

*I am abed. Forgive my weak hand, I have little strength. My limbs are drained of blood. My head is full of noises. The wound has worsened. I have an infection. That is what the doctor tells me. He could devote only a few moments to my cause. He has a hundred patients to see this morning, a hundred more in the afternoon, and there will be five hundred more still requiring his attention, their strength fading while they wait.*

*My dearest Susanna, my beloved wife, I would give anything to be beside you now, away from this forsaken place.*

*The flies are buzzing around me. A vulture circles overhead. Sergeant Fordham took a shot at him just now, but the round came straight back down to earth. Even if he had hit the vulture, its place would have been taken at once by another. They are everywhere hereabouts.*

*I am rambling. I must be to the point. I have not the time to waste.*

*My beloved wife, I must tell you one thing of great importance.*

*I was planning to keep it entirely to myself. But I may not be here for much longer. Better that you should know than the secret joins me in my grave.*

*Do you remember I wrote to you before about Tippoo's throne? I believe I said the eight tigers vanished and no one knows where.*

*My dearest wife, I lied. I know the whereabouts of those eight tigers. Seven of them have been taken by friends and comrades. I shall not transcribe their names here in case this letter falls into the wrong hands. I should not wish to incriminate them. I hope their fate will be happier than mine.*

*The eighth is mine. I do not have it on my person. I have hidden it in a safe place. I had been hoping to bring it home and sell it. With the proceeds, my sweet wife, we could have lived happily on a farm of our choosing. But I shall not see Cornwall again, nor Southampton, nor England, nor even tomorrow.*

*Two days after the battle was done, word came around that Wellesley would be searching the men's baggage for loot. Gold and silver, spoons and vases, all would be ignored, but awful punishments would befall anyone who was found to have secreted Tippoo's own treasures.*

*The next morning, I borrowed a fine horse from Hobson and left the camp at dawn.*

*I rode to the north. The roads were poor. I passed several small groups of men who gazed on me without fear or respect. Had I been afoot rather than riding a fine mare, they would surely have murdered me.*

*I had no notion of where I was headed, but I stayed on the same path, heading northwards all the time.*

*When the sun was directly overhead, I knew I must turn back soon, if I was to make the camp by nightfall.*

*I might have ridden twenty, or I might have ridden thirty miles, it was not easy to know. The landscape was so hilly and the roads so rough that any accurate figure is beyond me.*

*I cast about for a hiding place. I did not know what I was looking for. I knew simply that I must find somewhere that would hide an object for a few days till the hullabaloo had died down.*

*I had seen three villages, but no farms, no fields, noth-*

*ing like the ordered landscape of Hampshire that you know so well. This is a harsh country, filled with spiny trees and unscaleable boulders and prickly grasses. Snakes and lizards and other strange creatures lie in wait for unwary travellers, scuttling into the shade if they perceive you as a threat.*

*I saw a small hill which appeared not only uninhabited but unexplored. The Hindoos do not share our love of clambering up mountains simply to admire the view.*

*I spurred my horse and rode as far as I could, then dismounted and roped her reins to a tree. I continued on foot, stopping every few paces to catch my breath. I could see the scrubby landscape stretching for many miles behind me. The heat was brutal. A shimmering haze hid the horizon.*

*To my astonishment, I found a small shrine on the top of the hill. Someone had indeed been here before me. India is full of such places. The Hindoos have the strangest love of bizarre gods.*

*This pagan shrine was no more than a few golden bricks built around a hole in the ground. A dried-up well, perhaps, or a shelter from the sun, over which some Hindoo had placed this shrine and come to worship one of his strange gods.*

*I had already wrapped my tiger in my second-best shirt. Now I pushed aside the bricks and lowered myself into the hole.*

*I found a place there to hide the tiger. No one will find him. No one but you, my sweet wife.*

*I had not intended for you to retrieve him. I had hoped merely for the tiger to be safe there for a few days. Once the fear of looting had been forgotten, I could ride north and pluck him out again.*

*I should have sailed home to Southampton and handed him to you, my love. We would pick the rubies and diamonds and emeralds from his skin and sell them to the jewellers in Mercy Street and earn enough guineas to buy ourselves a small farm, where we might spend the rest of our days in quiet happiness. But my intentions have been dashed by the yellow pus now seeping out of my skin. The wound is infected. The contagion is spreading.*

*If Entwhistle were still here, I should ask him to bring the tiger to you himself, but he is buried already. His successor, Fordham, I do not trust, nor another man in the army, neither.*

*I shall give this letter to Captain Hobson. I have told him it is full of nothing but matters of love, and I must hope his curiosity does not lead him to break the seal.*

*I do not know how you will achieve it, my love, but you must bring yourself to India and find this tiger and use him to save yourself from poverty. He waits here for you. His jewels will guarantee the future of you and Thomas and Charlotte. With him, you will not suffer too much from my loss.*

*I cannot guarantee he will be there, of course. Someone may have found him. But I buried him well. And deep. I hope he shall remain undiscovered till you have a chance to dig him up.*

*Give my sweet children a hundred kisses every day from their father, and tell them how he loved them, and how he missed them, and how much he wished to see them.*

*I shall seal this letter now. Hobson has promised to visit me today. I shall make him swear to keep it on his person and deliver it into your gentle hands himself.*

*If you are reading these words, my dear Susanna, then I shall have been buried here, in the Hindoos' soil.*

*Please remember this: as I slipped away, I had only thoughts for you.*

*Your beloved husband,*

*Horatio Trelawney*

# 8

***So: now I understood*** what Grandpa had been selling. And now I knew why Marko was here.

These letters must be worth a lot more than two thousand euros.

I was pleased to discover that Horatio was a real Trelawney. I'd been worried from his letters that he might be more like my dad than my uncle. But now I knew he was as crafty as the rest of us.

Did Dad know about him? Or Uncle Harvey? If not, why not? And how had my grandfather discovered these letters? And, more important than anything else, where was the tiger?

If it had been rescued by Susanna or her kids or some other member of my family, wouldn't I have heard about it? And wouldn't we have been a bit richer?

A single sheet of paper was all that remained in the treasure box. It looked like a page torn from a notebook and was scrawled with a few words.

*I would rather live two days as a tiger than two hundred years as a sheep.*

*Tipu Sultan.*

*Jaragami.*

*Sotheby's Sale of 18th-century Indian and Islamic Art —3 March 2011—1.9m.*

The paper looked modern. The writing, too. I guessed it was my grandfather's.

But what did it mean?

Tipu Sultan must be Tippoo Sultan, the guy they'd been fighting in India. But who or what was Jaragami? Who or what was Sotheby's? And what about 1.9m? What was that?

It had to mean one point nine million.

Didn't it?

Was it true?

Could these letters really be worth two million dollars?

Of course they could. A two-hundred-year-old tiger covered in jewels—that couldn't be cheap.

Two million.

And Marko had offered me two thousand.

He could get lost.

I should fly to India and get the tiger myself.

But how?

I didn't have any money. How could I buy a flight? And what would I do when I got there? Like I said, I didn't know anything about India apart from the names of different curry dishes, and they wouldn't get me very far.

Maybe it didn't matter. India was just a country, right? It couldn't be too difficult to get around. Maybe I could borrow some money from Mom and Dad. I'd pay them back when I was a millionaire.

They'd never say yes.

Even if I stole some cash and used Dad's card to buy a plane ticket, I wouldn't know what to do once I got to India.

And what about Marko?

What if he was watching me? He'd see me walking out the door and grab me before I'd gotten anywhere near a plane, let alone as far as India.

So what was I going to do?

# 9

**Diamonds," said Uncle Harvey.**

"Just wait," I said.

"It gets better?"

"Much better."

"Good." He reached for the next letter in the pile, unfolded the crinkly browned paper, and started reading.

I'd already told him about the tiger, but he wanted to read the whole story for himself.

I had told him about Marko, too. Listening to my story of a thief breaking in to the house and tying me to the chair, Uncle Harvey had smiled. I suppose he thought I was joking around, trying to make my life sound more interesting than it actually was, taking revenge for the fact that I'd missed out on lunch. His smile got wider when I told him about the two thousand euros. Then I produced the book of letters and the smile was suddenly wiped from his face, replaced by an entirely different expression. I don't know what it was—greed? excitement?—but he glanced at the door to make sure it was closed, then told me to carry on.

Once I'd rattled through the rest of the story, he asked to read the letters. I said he could—on one condition. Whatever happened, whatever we made, two thousand or two million, we would split the proceeds fifty-fifty.

"We'll talk about money later," my uncle said. "Let me see the letters first."

"You can only see them if you agree about the money."

"I can't agree to anything till I've seen the letters."

"Fine," I said and folded my arms. "No deal."

"Oh, come on, Tom. You trust me, don't you?"

"Yes."

"So what's the problem?"

"There isn't a problem. I just want you to agree to a fifty-fifty split."

"What about expenses?"

"You'll have to pay mine now, because I don't have any money, but I'll pay you back as soon as I get my share."

My uncle hesitated for a moment and then nodded. He had nothing to lose. He held out his hand for the letters.

As he raced through them, he kept glancing at me, his eyes gleaming, as if he really hadn't expected to be having this much fun today.

I paced restlessly up and down Grandpa's bedroom. I could have gone through the letters myself, pointing out the juicy details to my uncle and filling in the gaps in the story, but he wanted to see it for himself. If he was going to join me in this escapade—if he was going to put up the cash for us to go to India and track down this tiger—then he had to be sure he wasn't wasting his time and money.

I couldn't have gone there myself. I didn't have a credit card. I knew nothing about India. But with my uncle's help, I could get there and find the tiger.

And earn a million dollars.

I stared out of the window at the gray mountains and wondered why Grandpa hadn't gone to India himself. Was he too old? Or didn't he have enough money? Something must have stopped him. I would have loved to know what. I would have liked to know how he discovered the letters, too. Had he always owned them but never bothered reading them? Or had he suddenly uncovered them, searching through an old box of junk, and seen immediately what they were worth?

Somehow he must have discovered the value of these letters and made contact with Marko and arranged to sell them. I wondered what price they had actually agreed on. Marko must have been lying about the two thousand euros. He would have thought he could cheat me. Grandpa wouldn't have been so easy.

A voice came from the other side of the room: "Tom, it's time to go." Dad was standing in the doorway, his arms folded.

"Go where?" I asked.

"The hotel," replied my father. "We'll have supper there,

then go to bed and carry on here in the morning. Harvey, where are you staying?"

"I don't know," said my uncle.

"I can ask at the hotel if they have another room."

"Don't bother. I'll be fine. I'll just sleep here."

Dad shrugged his shoulders. "Whatever you like." Then he turned to me. "Come on, Tom."

"I'd rather stay here too," I said.

"We're coming back in the morning," said Dad. "You can chat with Harvey then."

"He can stay if he wants to," said Uncle Harvey.

"That's sweet of you," said my dad. "But we don't want him running off to South America again."

"I promise you, Dad, I am not going to run off to South America."

"I know you're not. But even so, you can come and have supper with your mother and me."

"Why can't I stay here? I don't want to have to share a room with Jack and Grace. He snores and she'll spend the whole night texting. They won't want to share with me, either. It would be better for everyone if I stayed here."

"Where would you sleep?"

"On the sofa downstairs."

"It won't be comfortable."

"I don't mind. I can sleep anywhere."

"I don't think it's a very good idea."

By the way he said it, I knew he was wavering. With a bit more pressure, he might just crumble. He was probably still feeling guilty for banning me from Grandpa's funeral lunch. With any luck, I could play on that guilt and get what I wanted. I put on my best wheedling tone of voice. "Oh, come on, Dad. You know it makes sense. Jack and Grace will sleep much better. The room in the hotel won't be big enough for all three of us. Please, Dad."

Dad looked at his brother. "Will you look after him?"

"He's much more mature than I am."

"Sadly that's true," said Dad. He thought for a moment, then shrugged his shoulders. "If Mom says yes, I don't see why not. Come and talk to her. You're probably right about the room. Grace has been complaining about it already. She'll be happy, anyway. Good night, Harvey. See you tomorrow."

"Night, bro."

I followed Dad downstairs and we talked to Mom. I could see she didn't like the idea of me staying with Uncle Harvey, but she couldn't find any reason to say no. I fetched my bag from the back of the car, said good night to Jack and Grace, promised Mom and Dad that, yes, I would behave myself and, no, I wouldn't stay up too late, then said good night to them too and hurried back upstairs.

# 10

**Once Uncle Harvey had** read all the letters, he placed them carefully on the bed and smiled at me. "It's a great story. I like the sound of Horatio. I've heard of Tipu before, but I never knew much about him. And Wellesley, of course. You know who he is?"

"The general in charge of the army."

"Yes, but do you know who he became?"

"No."

"The Duke of Wellington. Heard of him?"

"Yes. He was, um . . ."

"Oh, come on, Tom. You must have heard of Wellington."

"I have. I just can't remember who he was."

"You've heard of Wellington boots?"

"Yes."

"They're named after him. And the battle of Waterloo? Wellington against Napoleon? You know who won that, don't you?"

"Wellington," I guessed.

"At least you know that much," said my uncle. "I really would have been shocked if you hadn't. You should read some books. Learn about history. 'Those who cannot remember the past are condemned to repeat it,' as the man said."

"Which man?"

"Santayana."

"Who?"

Uncle Harvey just laughed. Then he pulled out his phone and tapped the screen.

"What are you doing now?" I asked.

"Searching for information."

"About Wellington?"

"No, not about Wellington. About these tigers. Oh, it's so slow! The reception here is terrible."

He moved to the window and pointed his phone at the sky.

"Here we go," he said after a minute or two. "Ah, yes. This is the business."

"What is it?"

"A press release from Sotheby's."

"Oh, yeah. I wanted to ask you about that. What is Sotheby's?"

"Sotheby's is a very famous and respectable auction house. If you wanted to sell an antique tiger covered in jewels, you might well take it there."

"What do they say?"

"Have a look. It's from a sale of eighteenth- and nineteenth-century Indian art and antiques."

He turned the screen to me.

*The tiger was bought for $1,900,000 by a representative of the well-known Indian businessman and art collector Jalata Jaragami, who already owns six of the eight tigers from the famous throne. His unparalleled collection of historical material connected to Tipu Sultan will soon be on show to the public in a new museum to be built on the outskirts of Bangalore.*

I reached for his phone, wanting to scroll down and read more, but he snatched it back and started tapping the screen.

"What are you doing now?" I said.

"Searching."

"For what?"

"I told you: information."

"I didn't have to tell you about this," I said. "I could have done it on my own. We're partners now, Uncle Harvey. You've got to tell me what you're doing."

"Relax," he replied.

"No. Tell me. What are you searching for?"

"I've just typed in 'Jalata Jaragami tiger' and this is what I've found. Here you go—have a look."

It was an article from the *Hindustan Times.*

> Renowned entrepreneur and billionaire businessman Jalata Jaragami today announced the creation of a magnificent museum to house his collection of art, antiques, and relics connected to legendary ruler Tipu Sultan.

"I was born in Bengaluru and have lived in Karnataka for my entire life," said the owner of the Jaragami Corporation. "This is my small way of saying thank you and contributing something to the cultural heritage of my beloved local area."

The museum has been under construction for some time already, said Mr. Jaragami, and is due to open next year. Among the exhibits will be displayed one of Tipu Sultan's swords, a diamond brooch, and seven of the eight bejewelled tigers from Tipu's throne.

According to legend, Tipu Sultan ordered his craftsmen to build a magnificent throne, but swore a vow that he would not sit on it until the British had been banished from the sub-continent.

When Tipu Sultan's palace was overrun by the colonial East India army in May 1799, many of the treasures were looted and disappeared. Most were stolen by British soldiers and taken to their own country, some never to be seen again. Jalata Jaragami is determined to bring these valuables back to their home and gather Tipu Sultan's treasures in one place.

Uncle Harvey grabbed a sheet of paper from the bed. We looked at the words scrawled in my grandfather's shaky handwriting.

*I would rather live two days as a tiger than two hundred years as a sheep.*

*Tipu Sultan.*

*Jaragami.*

*Sotheby's Sale of 18th-century Indian and Islamic Art—3 March 2011—1.9m.*

"*This* guy really did pay two million dollars for it," muttered Uncle Harvey.

"Do you think he'll pay that much for the last tiger too?"

"I should be very surprised if he wouldn't pay even more."

"So, should we go and find it?"

"You don't even know it's still there."

"I bet it is."

"Why? What if Horatio's wife did as he suggested and found it for herself?"

"Wouldn't we know about that?"

"Maybe we would. Maybe we wouldn't. Even if she didn't, someone else might have done. Two hundred years is a long time for something to stay hidden."

"If it had been found, why would Marko be here?"

"Someone might have found it and kept it."

"Oh, come on, Uncle Harvey. You know it's still there, don't you? It's got to be! And we've got to go and find it. Let's go to India and get this tiger!"

"If only it was that easy."

"It is! Let's go there now!"

"You can't just go to India. I suppose we could try to buy tickets, but we'd also need visas or they wouldn't let us into the country."

"Couldn't we get one at the airport?"

"No."

"Why not?"

"Because that wouldn't be complicated enough. Everything in India is smothered in layers of bureaucracy. If you paid enough, you could probably get a visa in a day or two, but you'd still have to send your passport and a photo to the embassy."

"If we showed up in India without a visa, they couldn't send us home."

"They could and they would," said Uncle Harvey. "I tell you what, Tom. Leave this with me. I'll take the letters back to London and do some research. You remember my friend Theo? He's a professor at Edinburgh University, and he could—"

"The one who checked out John Drake's diaries?"

"That's him. He could find out if these letters are genuine. I've got an ex-girlfriend who works at Sotheby's. If she'll talk to me, she could put me in touch with the right people."

"Why wouldn't she talk to you?"

"We had a bad breakup. I ran off with her sister. But that's ancient history. I'm sure she's forgiven me. Anyway, with or without her, we'll do some research. If this whole thing is kosher, we could fly out to India and find the tiger."

"What about Marko?" I said.

"What about him?"

"He's searching for the tiger. He must be working for that businessman. Or he's planning to sell it to him. And if he's searching for the tiger, other people must be too. If we wait, it won't be there anymore. We have to go there now."

"I don't know."

I could see he was wavering. I just had to put a bit of pressure on him. I sat back and folded my arms. "You're right. Let's not get stressed about it. Anyway, it's only money, isn't it? What's a million dollars between friends?"

"A million dollars." My uncle wiped his lips with the back of his hand. "That would certainly solve a few problems."

"You need some money?"

"As it happens, I do."

"Then let's go and earn it. What are we waiting for? Let's get in your car and drive to the airport."

"That's a lovely idea, Tom, but it's just not practical."

"Why not?"

"What would your parents say?"

"I don't care about my parents."

"Fair enough. But what about tickets?"

"You could buy them over the Internet on your phone."

"You still haven't solved the problem of visas."

"I bet we can get them at the airport."

"I bet we can't."

"I bet we can," I repeated.

This time, he didn't argue. He just furrowed his brow, trying to think through the logistics.

"I could leave my rental car at the airport," he said. "What else? Let me think. Would I miss anything at home? I've got a couple of appointments next week, but I can change them." He turned to me. "What about you? When do you go back to the States?"

"We don't fly back till Thursday."

"This is crazy," said Uncle Harvey. But he started fiddling with his phone. "Let's see if there are any flights."

Ten minutes later, he had bought two tickets from Shannon to Bengaluru via Heathrow.

"Bengaluru?" I said. "I thought we were going to Bangalore."

"Bengaluru is Bangalore," explained my uncle. "The name has been changed."

"Why?"

"Over the past few years, names have been changed throughout India. Bombay has become Mumbai. Madras is now Chennai. They've thrown out the English names and replaced them with names which sound more Indian. Supposedly they're throwing off the shackles of colonialism, but most people seem to carry on using the old names anyway, the ones they know."

"So what should I call it, Bangalore or Bengaluru?"

"That's entirely up to you."

There was lots of space on the first leg of the journey, Ireland to England, so the tickets weren't too pricey, but the flight from England to India had only two free seats, and each of them cost $2700. Our return flights would take us directly home to the States. If we were lucky, that would give us enough time to find the tiger. If we weren't lucky . . .

"We have to be lucky," said Uncle Harvey. "I need the money. If we don't find the tiger, I won't be able to pay my debts."

"Debts? I thought you were rich."

"Sadly not."

"What about the money you got from John Drake's diary?"

"I lost it playing poker."

When Uncle Harvey and I went to Peru together, we were searching for a vast hoard of gold and silver buried there by Sir Francis Drake in the 1500s. I'm not going to tell you the whole story now, but I will tell you that Uncle Harvey came back home with a nice payoff from the Peruvian government. I said, "You can't have lost all that money."

"I did," replied Uncle Harvey. "And more."

"How can you lose more money than you've got?"

"All too easily. I owe ninety grand to one of the guys who was sitting around the table. He wants it back. In fact, he threatened to break both my legs with a baseball bat if I don't pay him by the end of next week. So let's hope the tiger is still there."

# 11

**I wrote a note** for Mom and Dad and left it on the kitchen table.

*Hi, Mom and Dad, I've gone out with Uncle Harvey. Back soon. Love from Tom.*

I should have told them the truth, but I wanted to give myself a little extra time in case they arrived early in the morning, discovered what I was doing, and tried to get me removed from the flight.

We walked out of the house and closed the front door quietly behind us. The night was cold and clear. Stars sparkled overhead, but there wasn't a single light burning in any of the other windows in the village.

We got in the car and drove away. I took one last look at the house, trying to imagine Mom and Dad arriving in the morning. What would they do? Wander through the rooms, calling out my name? Or go straight to the kitchen and find my note? When they read what I'd written, would they believe me? Or would they think Uncle Harvey and I had gone back to Peru?

I felt bad, leaving them again. Well, I felt bad about leaving Mom. She'd been really upset last time. Dad had mostly just been mad, which Mom said was his way of showing he cared. Yeah, right. However, I have to admit, I only felt bad for about a second. Then I remembered Marko and the tiger and all the fun I was going to have in India, and I thought, *It's time to go! We've got to make that plane before Mom and Dad figure out that I'm gone.*

We'd been driving for ten or fifteen minutes when my uncle said, "I don't suppose you know what type of car your friend Marko drives?"

"No idea," I replied. "Why?"

"Just wondering."

As he said those words, my uncle's eyes flicked to the rearview mirror.

I turned around and saw a pair of headlights following us through the country lanes.

I said, "Do you think it's Marko?"

"Probably not."

"How long has he been there?"

"Since we left the village."

"He must have been watching the house."

"It might just be a coincidence."

"I bet you anything it's Marko."

Uncle Harvey didn't argue. Instead he put his foot down and accelerated around a bend. The tires screeched. A startled fox stood by the side of the road, its eyes glistening in our headlights.

We drove fast for five minutes. The other car stayed with us.

My uncle slowed down, giving them a chance to overtake, but they didn't take it. He sped up again and so did they. Whatever we did, the distance between us remained the same.

"What are we going to do?" I asked.

"Nothing."

"Why not?"

"What *can* we do?"

"We could pull over and wait for him to stop, then jump out and slash his tires."

"Nice plan," said Uncle Harvey. "Have you ever done anything like that before?"

"No."

"I have. It's a lot more difficult than it sounds. And we know he has a knife. What if he has a gun, too? No, we'll just drive. Let's see if he follows us all the way to Shannon."

"What if he follows us all the way to India?"

"We'll think of something."

I was disappointed. I would have preferred to stop and confront Marko. But maybe Uncle Harvey was right. What if he did have a gun? What if he shot us and stole the letters? We'd feel pretty stupid. That is, if we were alive long enough to feel anything.

I said, "When did you slash someone's tires?"

"Oh, it's a long story."

"I'm not going anywhere."

Uncle Harvey laughed. "Fine. I'll tell you."

It *was* a long story, but a good one—it involved an Italian countess, a French politician, and a suitcase full of fake dollars. I can't tell you any more than that, because Uncle Harvey swore me to secrecy. Apparently the politician is now one of the most powerful men in Europe and if he discovered I was telling stories about his past, he'd track me down and wipe me out.

Just before the airport, we pulled into a gas station. You have to return rental cars with a full tank of gas, Uncle Harvey told me. Otherwise the rental company charges you a fortune for filling it up.

The station was deserted. A cashier stared at us through the big glass window, then went back to watching TV, waiting for us to come and pay for our gas. Uncle Harvey unclipped the hose and filled the tank.

A second car purred into the gas station. Once again, the clerk lifted his head, took a quick look, then went back to the TV.

It was a Ford Focus, no different from the one we'd gotten from Shannon airport, and for a horrible moment I thought Dad might be driving. Had he been waiting outside the house, expecting us to sneak away? Was he now going to confront us? No. He must be safely tucked up in his hotel bedroom. It was Marko sitting behind the wheel.

I could see his eyes fixed on me.

I turned away. Turned back.

He was still watching me.

I was scared of him. I don't mind admitting that. Otherwise I would have waved the letters out the window and said, *They're ours now! Thanks for your offer of two thousand, but no thanks! I'll take the two million.*

But I didn't say anything. Nor did I move from my seat.

Uncle Harvey paid for the gas and walked back to the car. I could see him looking at Marko.

He opened the door and peered down at me. "That's the guy?"

"That's him."

Uncle Harvey straightened up and took a long look.

The clerk was watching us from his booth. He must have been wondering why we weren't continuing with our journey and why Marko was just sitting in his car, not buying any gas.

"Let's go and see what he wants," said Uncle Harvey. He slammed the door and headed for Marko's car.

I jumped out of the car and ran after him. "Wait!"

He turned around to look at me. "What?"

"You said we shouldn't confront him."

"I've changed my mind."

"What if he has a gun?"

"We'll be fine." Uncle Harvey gestured at the booth. "He won't dare shoot us here. Everything's being recorded on the security camera."

By now, Marko was ready for us. He'd stepped out of his

car and was standing with his arms folded, waiting to see what we did next.

Uncle Harvey started walking.

I shouted after him again: "Wait!"

He didn't.

I didn't like it. Marko was dangerous. Ruthless, too. What if he drew a gun or a knife? What if he didn't care about being recorded or getting caught?

I ran after my uncle and caught up with him just as he reached Marko.

Uncle Harvey didn't bother with small talk. "Why are you following us?"

"You know why," replied Marko.

"You're wasting your time," said my uncle. "We're keeping the letters."

"Didn't he"—he pointed at me—"tell you what I'm offering for them?"

"He said you'd offered two thousand euros."

"That's right."

"Not much if they lead to a tiger worth two million dollars."

"Yeah, but you'll never find it."

"We'll take that risk."

"Let me tell you something, mate. J.J. has hundreds of people searching for this tiger. They've been all over India, Europe, America, and they haven't found a trace of it. You won't either."

"But you will?" I blurted out.

"I might, yes. I know what I'm doing. I've also got a bit of money to spend. Which is why I'd like to buy your father's letters. He was a good bloke, your dad. I liked him."

"How did you meet him?"

"He got in touch with my boss. Said he had something to sell. We still want to buy it. Are you going to honor the deal we made?"

"I don't think so," said Uncle Harvey.

"I'm sorry to hear that, mate. Why not?"

"Because the tiger is worth at least two million dollars and you offered two thousand euros. That's a big difference."

"I offered two thousand for the letters, not the tiger."

"Even so."

"You want more money?" asked Marko.

"Of course."

"How much?"

"What are you offering?" said my uncle.

"If you can give me the letters right now, I'll pay you twenty thousand euros."

"Twenty thousand?" I knew I should shut up, but I couldn't help myself. He'd offered me two! Would he have gone up to twenty if I'd asked him?

He grinned at me. He must have known what I was thinking. And he said, "That's right. Twenty thousand euros. In cash."

My uncle said, "Do you have the money here?"

"Yes."

"With you?"

"Yes."

"In your car?"

"Yes."

Uncle Harvey took a moment to decide. He glanced at Marko's car as if he was imagining the money inside. Where would it be? In a suitcase? Or an envelope? What does twenty thousand euros actually look like? How much space does it take up? Then he shook his head. "I'm afraid the answer's no. Twenty thousand is simply not enough."

"No problem," said Marko. "I'll give you thirty."

"No."

"Thirty-five. That's my final offer."

"You can have them for a million," said Uncle Harvey.

Marko laughed. "Come on, mate! Don't be ridiculous."

"That's *my* final offer."

"You're making a big mistake."

"Maybe I am. Maybe I'm not. But it's my mistake to make, not yours. We're going to leave now. Please don't follow us anymore."

Marko reached into his jacket. My uncle tensed. So did I. We both thought he was reaching for a gun. But he pulled out his wallet. "Here's my card. Call me if you change your mind."

"I will." Uncle Harvey glanced at the card. "Malinkovic—where's that from?"

"I'm Australian, but my dad emigrated from Croatia."

"A wonderful country."

"I've never been."

"You should. It's beautiful." Uncle Harvey pocketed the card. "Nice to meet you, Marko. Let's keep in touch."

"We'll do that, mate."

We walked back to our car. The gas station attendant was still watching us. I was glad about that. He and his cameras might just have saved our lives. If Marko had produced his knife and swung at us, could we have stopped him?

We got into the car and drove out of the gas station.

As we roared up the access road onto the freeway, I turned around and saw the Ford Focus following right behind us.

I lifted my hand and waved at Marko.

He didn't wave back.

I turned to my uncle.

"J.J.," I said.

"I noticed that too."

"That's got to be Jalata Jaragami, doesn't it?"

"Must be."

"Do you really think he's got hundreds of people searching for this tiger?"

"I don't see why not. If he wants to find it badly enough."

"So who's Marko?"

"Why don't you look him up?" He passed me his phone and the card that Marko had given him.

The card had his full name, Marko Malinkovic, two phone numbers, and a Gmail address, but no information about his job, his title, who he was, or what he did for a living.

I searched for "Marko Malinkovic." It was an unusual

name, so he should have been easy to follow, but he had no Facebook page, no Twitter account, no website advertising his business or offering his services. He hadn't told the world his hobbies or posted images of himself partying with his friends. Whoever he was, he liked to keep himself private.

I found a few Malinkovics in Melbourne, Australia. There was a Zeljko Malinkovic who sold homemade cakes with guaranteed fresh cream and a Steve Malinkovic who had a garage on Silver Street specializing in German cars. Could they be his parents? His brothers and sisters?

"Maybe Malinkovic isn't even his real name," suggested my uncle. "But don't worry about it. Marko doesn't really matter. Forget him. He's out of the picture."

"No, he's not. He's right behind us."

"He might be now, but he won't be for long. Like I said, you should forget him. The guy we need to meet is J.J."

# 12

***I would have been happy*** to forget Marko, but he refused to be forgotten. He was on our flight to Heathrow.

He had followed us all the way to the Shannon airport, keeping a safe distance between his car and ours, then dropped away and disappeared once we reached the car rental place. We didn't see him again in the airport, but he must have followed us inside, watched us checking in, discovered where we were going, and bought a ticket for himself.

He sat at the other end of the plane. I thought of going back there and talking to him, asking him to leave us alone, but Uncle Harvey told me not to bother. "We'll shake him off later," he said.

"What if we can't?"

"We will."

"How do you know? He's followed us all the way here. He'll probably be able to follow us all the way to India. What if we find the tiger and he grabs it from us?"

"Relax, Tom. We'll be fine. He's just one guy. He can't do anything to us."

"There might be others. He might have a whole team. Maybe they're waiting for us at Heathrow. What if they mug us and grab the letters?"

"Didn't I tell you to relax? Shut up and read your magazine."

Uncle Harvey had bought me a copy of *History Today* in a shop at the airport. I said I wasn't interested in boring magazines about dead people, but he told me not to be so narrow-minded. "You're interested in Tipu's tigers, aren't you?"

"Yes, but—"

"And you were interested in John Drake's diaries? And Francis Drake's gold?"

"That's not the same as—"

"Read the magazine," he said. "You might learn something. Even better, you might find someone else who buried some treasure for us to go and dig up."

I flicked through the pictures and read a couple of the articles. They were actually pretty interesting, even if they didn't give me any ideas for how or where to make my fortune.

We landed at Heathrow and switched terminals. The last time I saw Marko, he was standing in a line at passport control, staring angrily after us. Our line moved much faster than his and he was still waiting while we were hurrying into the main part of the airport. Once again, I lifted my arm and waved at him. Once again, he didn't wave back.

Uncle Harvey stopped at a cash machine and pulled three cards from his wallet. Each of them allowed him to take out five hundred pounds.

"That should keep us going for a few days," he said.

"I thought you didn't have any money."

"I don't."

"So how can you get out all this cash?"

"That's the definition of a credit card," said Uncle Harvey. "Buy now, pay later. I already owe about ten thousand bucks on mine."

"Plus ninety thousand from your poker game."

"And a few thousand here and there for other debts to other people too."

"If you added it all up, how much would it be?"

"I don't know and I don't want to know. Life is too short. Anyway, you don't have to worry about my financial situation. When we find this tiger, all our problems will be over."

"What if we don't?"

"Then I'll have to run away and start a new life under a different name."

"What about me?"

"You'll be fine. You don't owe anything to anyone. Apart from me, and I'll forgive you."

He had another card in his wallet that got him free entry to the British Airways executive lounge. We bagged a couple of sofas and lay down. Our flight left in nine hours. There was nothing to do till then but snooze.

"Good night," said Uncle Harvey.

"What about Marko?"

"What about him?"

"What if he finds us? What if he comes in here while we're sleeping? What if he steals the bag?"

"Even if he finds us, which he probably won't, he can't steal the bag. She'll be watching us." Uncle Harvey nodded at the woman sitting behind the reception desk. Now I understood why he had chosen the sofa directly in her line of sight. "Anyway, I'm a light sleeper." He was using his bag as a pillow and had looped its straps through his wrists. No one would be able to get near the zip without disturbing him.

"When do we have to wake up?" I said.

"Don't worry about that. I've set my alarm. Now get some sleep. You're going to need all your energy when you get to India."

He lay down. So did I.

I tried to sleep. I really did. But I lay awake for a long time, worrying about Marko. I remembered his dark eyes, the glint of his knife, and the menacing tone in his voice. Where was he now? Pacing around Heathrow, searching for us? Wouldn't he find us here? Would that woman at the desk really protect us? I knew I wouldn't find the answers to any of these questions, but they spun around my head until I finally fell asleep.

# 13

**I was woken by Uncle Harvey** shaking my shoulder. He thrust a cup at me. "Drink this," he said. "You'll feel better."

"What is it?"

"Coffee."

"You know I don't like coffee."

"Don't be an idiot. Everyone likes coffee."

"I don't."

"Try it."

"No, thanks."

"Fine. I'll drink them both."

He took a sip from one cup, then the other.

I sat up, rubbing my eyes. A different woman was sitting at the desk. She smiled at me. I smiled back.

The bag was still sitting on the sofa beside Uncle Harvey. So we hadn't been robbed. That was good.

I pulled my phone from my pocket. A text had arrived while I was asleep.

**Where are you? Please come back and help clean this house. Mom.**

Should I ignore it? No. Better to reply now and keep her off the trail. I tapped in a quick message.

**Back soon. Tom**

I pressed Send and switched off my phone.

We gathered our gear and left the lounge. I searched for Marko as we walked through the airport, but I didn't see him anywhere. He wasn't in the line to get on the plane. But that didn't mean he wasn't there. He could have been up at the front in first class.

Once we were airborne, I unbuckled my seat belt and stood up. "I'll be back in a second." I didn't know what I was planning to say to Marko if I found him. Would I run back and get Uncle Harvey? Or confront him myself? I hadn't thought that far ahead. First I wanted to discover if he was here.

"Where are you going?" asked my uncle.

"To the bathroom."

"You went just before we boarded. What's wrong with you?"

"Nothing."

"Do you have a bladder infection?"

"No. I just need to pee. I've been drinking a lot of water."

He gave me a quizzical look, then returned his attention to the *Sunday Times.*

Why didn't I tell the truth? I guess I didn't want to be told to relax again. I'm relaxed enough already. I just don't enjoy being followed around by psychopaths with knives. I prefer to know about it if they're on the same plane as me.

I snuck into first class. The flight attendant gave me a stern look, but I just smiled and she didn't stop me or tell me to go back to the cheap seats where I belonged.

Marko wasn't there.

We'd escaped.

Or had we?

Would he know where we were going? Could he find out? He could get on the next plane. He might be a few hours behind us, but that wouldn't matter to him. He could call a friend or an armed heavy and tell him to wait for our flight. He'd watch out for us as we emerged from the airport and follow us wherever we went, and we'd never know he was there, because we wouldn't know who he was or what he looked like.

I went back to my seat and settled down for the rest of the journey. Uncle Harvey was halfway through a plastic cup of something fizzy. I said, "What's that?"

"Gin and tonic. You want one?"

"Yes, please."

He grinned and shook his head. "You're too young for gin."

"I'm old enough to try."

"No, you're not. But I'll give you a tip for when you're older. Always drink gin on a plane. It sends you straight to sleep. In fact, I think I need another." He tipped the rest of the glass down his throat and waved at the nearest flight attendant.

# 14

***The gin did its job*** and Uncle Harvey soon fell asleep. I wasn't tired, so I just sat there, playing with the in-flight entertainment system and eating the free spicy peanuts. I just wanted to get there and start hunting for treasure.

We landed at one o'clock in the morning, local time. As we walked out of the air-conditioned aircraft and into the terminal, I pulled off my sweater and tied it around my waist. Even at this time of the night, the heat was astonishing. My bag was stuffed with sweaters, jeans, and thick socks, perfect for Irish mountains, but dead weight here.

I switched on my phone. It took five minutes to work out where it was. The poor thing must have been very confused. Home, England, Ireland, India—where was it now? When the display finally bleeped into life, a text arrived from the phone company, telling me the charges to make and receive calls, swiftly followed by seven voice mails from Mom and Dad. They started angry and quickly got panicked. I'd have to call them back. But what would I say? How much of the truth should I tell? I put the phone away and added that to the list of things to think about later.

When we reached the front of the line, the passport officer turned the pages of my passport, then Uncle Harvey's. "You are father and son?"

"Uncle and nephew," Harvey replied.

"What is the purpose of your visit?"

"We're on holiday."

"Where is your visa?"

"I'm afraid we don't have visas," said Uncle Harvey.

"For visiting India, you must have a visa."

"I know. Where can we buy them?"

"The best place to get a visa is the embassy in your capital city at least one month before you are arriving in India."

"We're here now," replied Uncle Harvey. "We don't mind paying. Where do we go to buy our visas?"

"That is not possible," said the passport officer. "You must return to your own country and purchase a visa. Then you may enter India."

Uncle Harvey reached into his jacket and pulled out his wallet. He opened it up to show the bills inside. He didn't actually pull out any money—he wasn't that blatant—but he made it obvious what was on offer. "There must be some way for us to get a visa," he said.

"That is not possible."

"Really? Why not?"

"Because there are rules and regulations governing every

aspect of entrance and exit from this country. The rules are stating most clearly that all visitors must have a visa."

Uncle Harvey fingered the money. "We're here now and we really need these visas. We don't mind paying for them. Couldn't you see if you could help us? Please?"

The passport officer thought for a moment. He cast a few glances around, checking to see if he was being watched. "There is a possibility," he said in a quiet voice. "But it is very expensive."

"That doesn't matter," said Uncle Harvey.

"You will come with me, please."

The passport officer spoke to one of his colleagues, who took his position, then led us through a maze of corridors to a windowless room crammed with tired, anxious people. One woman was weeping silently into a handkerchief, her shoulders shuddering. The passport officer wrote our names on a sheet of paper and asked for ten thousand rupees. Uncle Harvey didn't have any local currency, but the passport officer was happy to accept British pounds instead. He counted the notes, folded them carefully, and slid them into the top pocket of his jacket. Then he told us to wait.

I said, "For how long?"

He just smiled and walked away.

"What if he never comes back?" I said.

"He will," replied my uncle.

"How do you know?"

"He had a good face. I trust him."

I hoped he was right. What if the passport officer decided to keep our money and pretend he'd never met us? We wouldn't be able to prove anything. We'd sit here for a day or two, sweltering, then they'd shove us on a plane back to London.

Uncle Harvey found a newspaper lying on the floor, the pages covered in dusty footprints. We were just settling down to read it when his phone rang. He looked at the display.

"It's your father," he said. "Do you want to talk to him?"

"No."

"You should."

"I haven't decided what to say."

"It's always best to tell the truth."

"I can't do that!"

"Of course you can." He put the phone to his ear. "Hello, Simon. I'm fine, thanks. Yes, he is. He's right here, I'll pass you over."

I took the phone. "Hi, Dad."

"Where are you?" said my father.

"India," I replied.

"Where?"

"India," I repeated.

"Where's that?"

"It's a big country near China."

"Don't be funny with me, Tom. Where are you?"

"I just told you. I'm in India."

"How can you be in India? How did you get there?"

"On a plane."

There was a pause. Then Dad said: "Is this true?"

"Yes."

"You're really in India?"

"Yes."

"Where?"

"Bangalore."

"You are in serious trouble."

"I don't care."

"I mean it. You are in very serious trouble."

"Whatever."

I could hear the steam coming out of his ears.

"Hand the phone to your uncle."

"Sure."

I handed the phone to Uncle Harvey. I could only hear one side of their conversation, but I could fill in the rest for myself. Dad asked what we were doing in India and Uncle Harvey said he'd explain when we got home again. Dad asked when that would be and Uncle Harvey said he wasn't quite sure. Dad said he would call the police and Uncle Harvey asked him not to. It carried on like that for a couple more minutes, back and forth, back and forth, and then Uncle Harvey ended the call. He shook his head. "Your father needs to learn how to relax."

"Was he any different when you were kids?"

"Exactly the same."

I slumped in my plastic chair, praying to myself that we would find the tiger so I could return home with enough money to placate Mom and Dad.

I'd buy them a new house.

A couple of cars.

The best vacation of their lives.

They'd have to forgive me.

They'd have to.

And if they didn't?

I'd never come home. I'd have enough to live alone. I'd hire a cook and a chauffeur. Forget school. I'd be like Uncle Harvey. I'd travel around the world, searching for treasure and having adventures.

I was lost in imaginings of my future life, alone and free and rich and happy, when Uncle Harvey's phone rang again. This time it was Mom. She insisted on speaking to me. Not bothering with any small talk, she said, "Is it true?"

"Is what true?"

"Are you in India?"

"Yes."

"What are you doing there?"

I told her everything. Well, not all the details about the treasure. We were in a crowded room and anyone might have been listening. But I told her enough that she'd understand why we had no choice about jumping on a plane and coming to India.

"Oh, Tom," said Mom.

"You don't have to worry about me," I said. "Everything's going to be fine."

"When are you coming home?"

"I don't know. Soon."

"Why don't you just come home now?"

"I don't want to."

"But, Tom . . ." she sighed. Then she told me to be careful, and said she loved me, and that was that. She just ended the call. No threats to get the police involved. No shouting or screaming. Just me alone in India with Uncle Harvey, and Mom and Dad and Grace and Jack halfway around the world, soon to be on their way home. I was so glad I wasn't with them.

# 15

***We sat in that room*** for a long time.

It was hot and boring.

Nothing happened.

Most people were dozing. Others just stared into space. One family had made a little shelter for themselves, hanging clothes and blankets over the chairs, as if they expected to be here for several days, or already had been.

At some point, I must have fallen asleep.

I was woken by Uncle Harvey poking me in the ribs.

The passport officer was standing over us, holding both our passports. He thrust them into my uncle's hands and smiled.

"Welcome to India, Mr. and Mr. Trelawney."

# 16

**At a booth in the main part** of the airport, Uncle Harvey changed some British pounds into Indian rupees. Then we went to find a taxi. It was still early in the morning, but we were going to head straight to the station and get a train to Mysore. From there, we'd take another taxi to Srirangapatna—as Seringapatam is now called. Then we'd head north, following Horatio's instructions, searching for the hill where he'd buried Tipu's tiger.

Indians have two types of taxi, Uncle Harvey told me: cars and rickshaws. Both sorts were packed outside the airport, waiting for passengers. The cars looked like normal cars, just older. The rickshaws were little three-wheelers, half-motorbike, half-van, with a driver sitting alone at the front and a seat in the back with room for a couple of passengers. I would have liked to ride in one, but Uncle Harvey said they were only good for short journeys. They had no doors or windows, and nowhere to put luggage, so you had to keep your bag at your feet or on your knees.

He must have seen my disappointment, because he told

me not to worry. "We're going to be here for a few days," he said. "You'll definitely get the chance to ride in a rickshaw."

Once we were sitting in the back seat of a yellow taxi, Uncle Harvey called forward. "Hello? Excuse me? Could you turn on the meter, please?"

"Yes, sir. No problem." The driver tapped the meter and the dials reverted to a line of zeros. If he hadn't done that, we would have had to pay the last passenger's fare on top of ours. I didn't know that at the time, but Uncle Harvey gave me a few tips on surviving India, and dealing with taxis was number four on the list. In case you're wondering about the others, number one was toilets, number two was water, and number three was food, and his advice was 1) always squat, 2) only drink bottled, and 3) be very careful what you eat.

The driver said to my uncle: "What is your destination, sir?"

"The railway station."

"Coming right up, sir."

As we sped away from the terminal, I peered out of the back window, searching for Marko. If he'd been quick enough, the time we spent in the visa department would have given him a chance to catch up with us, taking a flight here via Mumbai or Delhi. Even if he hadn't managed to get a ticket on another flight, had he called his friends who lived here? Or had he told J.J.'s other thugs to watch out for us? Had we been followed as we emerged from the airport?

I was just in time to see a second car peeling away from the lines of taxis. It stayed a steady distance behind us as we drove down the road. Of course it did. We were heading out of the airport and into the center of the city. Wouldn't anyone take the same route?

I told my uncle what I'd seen. I'd imagined he would tell me to relax, but he actually turned around and stared thoughtfully at the taxi.

"Did you see Marko?" asked my uncle.

"I couldn't see who was inside. Do you think it's him?"

"Almost certainly not. But let's still keep an eye on it."

The taxi stayed with us as we drove over a bridge, but fell behind as soon as we joined a larger highway, fading into the mass of cars and trucks jamming the road, and we soon lost sight of it.

That seemed to satisfy my uncle, but I couldn't help worrying about Marko. What if he followed us to Mysore, waited for us to find the tiger, and then grabbed it from us? We'd have done all the hard work and he'd walk away with the reward. I glanced behind us every few moments all the way to the station, trying to work out if we were being followed. I saw lots of taxis, but I didn't know if any of them was the particular taxi that had left the airport at the same time as us.

We stopped at some traffic lights. Immediately our taxi was surrounded by kids. They pushed stuff against the glass, trying to persuade us to buy sweets or drinks or newspapers. The driver waved them away like flies, but they took no notice, rapping their knuckles against the glass, trying to get our attention.

There were more kids at every subsequent set of lights, selling more sweets and drinks and trinkets and newspapers and magazines. Often they didn't even need to wait till we came to a red light; the traffic moved so slowly that they could just run alongside us, knocking on the glass, shouting a few words of English at us: *Hello, sir! Please, sir! You will buy, sir? You will take one, sir? Only one rupee! Very good price!* When the lights changed and the taxi started moving, the kids leaped aside, dodging through the cars and stepping onto the safety of the pavement, where they stood patiently, chatting, laughing, passing the time, waiting for the lights to go red again and give them another chance to earn some money. I'd seen some movies about India and they'd all shown scenes like these, kids crowding around cars, trying to earn a little money, but the reality was completely different from watching it on a screen. In a movie, India looked cute and fun and unusual and exciting. Up close, it looked grubby and depressing. These kids weren't having fun. They were just trying to scrape together a few pennies to buy themselves something to eat. I asked Uncle Harvey for some money to give them, but he said no.

"Why not?"

"When you come to India, you have to make a choice. Do you give money to everyone? Or no one? It's up to you."

"Couldn't I just give some to those kids?"

"No."

After about an hour of this, the driver stopped his taxi, turned around, and grinned at us. "Here is our destination, sir. Bangalore Main Terminus. The charge will be ninety-seven rupees."

Uncle Harvey pointed at the meter. "It says thirty-seven."

"Airport charge, sir. Fifty rupees."

"That makes eighty-seven."

"Also ten rupees must be charged for crossing the city boundary."

"That's ridiculous."

"It is the rules and regulations, sir. Here, I will show you."

The driver reached into his glove compartment and pulled out a sheaf of papers.

While he and Uncle Harvey were arguing about the price, I opened my door and stepped out of the car. The sun had risen higher and the heat was even more intense. The air smelled of spices. The road was four lanes wide and busier than a highway, filled with traffic moving at unbelievable speed. Pedestrians nipped between the cars. How could anyone cross this road? I saw a crosswalk, but it was obviously only for decoration, because the cars didn't bother stopping for anyone walking across it. Pedestrians just had to run. Someone jostled me. I gripped my bag tighter. A man tugged my sleeve. "You want good movie?" He offered a sheaf of pirated DVDs. I couldn't bring myself to answer. I don't know why not. I guess I was stunned. I'd never been anywhere like this, never seen streets that were so busy, so full of noise and movement, packed with so many smells and colors.

The DVD salesman was still tugging my sleeve and asking questions, but I heard another voice that was louder than his: "Come on! This way!" My uncle was already on the move. I pushed past the DVD guy and hurried after him.

The street might have been crowded, but the station was crammed. We had to fight our way through the entrance, pushing past porters carrying luggage, kids selling newspapers, and people hurrying in every direction, shouting and hugging and laughing and pushing and generally getting in one another's way. No one apologized for treading on my toes. No one stepped out of my way. Soon I found myself struggling as hard as everyone else. I didn't want to get separated from my uncle. I knew I'd never find him again.

A voice boomed out the times, destinations, and platforms of various trains. Beggars were everywhere, stretching out their hands. Some were missing arms, others had no legs, and I saw one who didn't have any limbs at all, just four stumps sticking out of his body.

"You give me money," demanded one of the beggars, a kid about my age with a flapping sleeve where his right arm should have been. I mumbled some kind of apology and hurried past.

Now I understood what my uncle had said in the car. How could we give a coin to one of these beggars and not the others? How could we choose who was worthy of our charity? But wouldn't it be better to give some money to one of them rather than none at all?

I thought of my home, my possessions, my clothes, the food that appeared on our table every day, the big bags that

Mom brought home from the supermarket once a week, and I wasn't sure whether to feel guilty or grateful that I was born in America rather than here.

At the ticket office, we were greeted by a long line snaking down the corridor. We shuffled slowly toward the booths. Women fanned their faces with newspapers, men grumbled and sweated.

A couple of skinny boys walked up and down the line, carrying buckets and calling out, "Chai! Chai! Chai!"

They were selling tea, my uncle told me. Inside their buckets they had metal teapots and little glasses, and sold the tea already mixed with milk and sugar. There was nothing better in this hot weather, said Uncle Harvey, than a cup of hot, sweet tea. It cooled you down more effectively than any number of cold drinks. "It's called chai," he explained. "That's the Indian word for tea. Do you want to try it?"

I said I didn't like tea, but Uncle Harvey insisted on buying me a cup, and another for himself.

I took a sip. To my surprise, it wasn't bad. Even more surprisingly, it did seem to cool me down.

The kid with the bucket carried on down the line, then returned to collect our empty cups.

When we reached a ticket booth, my uncle said, "When is the next train to Mysore?"

"The Udyan Express leaves in twenty-three minutes."

"Two tickets, please. Second class."

"At this late notice, it is not possible to have a reservation."

"That's fine, thank you. We'll find a seat ourselves."

The clerk gave a little sigh, as if he was disappointed about the reservations even if we weren't, then printed out our tickets.

Uncle Harvey handed over a sheaf of dirty banknotes, then took the tickets and his change. "Where do we go to get the train?"

"You must proceed immediately to platform eighteen. The express is boarding already. You must hurry, sir."

"Thanks!"

Uncle Harvey grabbed our tickets and the change.

We sped through the station. My uncle was taller than me, and bigger, too, so the crowd parted to let him through. What if I got left behind? What if we were separated? I was struggling to keep up with him when someone grabbed my arm.

I tried to shake them off.

They wouldn't let go.

One of those beggars asking for money.

*Sorry, pal. Don't have any. Try someone else. Get off my arm.*

He wouldn't let go.

I shook harder.

He still didn't let go.

I turned around, ready to tell him I didn't have any rupees, and found myself face-to-face with Marko.

He was holding me with his left hand. His right hand was under his jacket, gripping something dark and angular and metallic. I could see just enough to know it was a gun.

# 17

**Call your uncle," Marko said.** "Tell him to come back here."

"What do you—?"

"Do it!"

"No." I don't know what made me so brave. Maybe it was jetlag, or maybe just stupidity, but for whatever reason, I tried to pull myself free. "Get off me."

"I've got a gun," said Marko.

"You can't shoot me here."

"I can. And I will."

"You wouldn't dare."

"That's what your grandfather said just before I killed him. I'll do the same to you if you don't call your uncle."

I felt myself shivering. I don't know if I was scared or furious. Had he really killed Grandpa? Could he be telling the truth? I didn't know much about the way my grandfather had actually died. Only what Mom had told me. How much did she actually know, though? Had the police investigated? Probably not. If an old man has a heart attack in front of the TV, you probably don't bother searching for clues. You wouldn't think he'd been murdered by a thug on the trail of some old letters.

Marko must have seen that I was about to throw myself at him, because he jabbed the gun into my chest and said in a low voice, "Call your uncle. Now."

"Did you really kill him?"

"Call him now or I'll kill you, too."

There was something in his eyes that told me he was serious. I turned my head and yelled, "Uncle Harvey!"

He'd managed to get halfway across the station and didn't hear me.

I shouted louder: "Uncle Harvey!"

He was moving quickly through the crowd, leaving me behind. Another moment or two and he'd be gone forever. I'd be stuck in the middle of Bangalore Station with a million beggars and an angry Aussie with a gun.

I took a deep breath and made the most noise that I'd ever made in my life: "UNCLE HARVEY!"

That made him stop. He turned around. I could see the different expressions crossing his face: irritation, astonishment, anger.

Then he was pushing back through the crowd, heading toward us.

Marko positioned himself behind me. For a moment, he let go of my arm, and I thought, *This is it, I've got to run.* But before I had a chance to move, I felt the end of his gun nudging the middle of my back.

Could he really shoot me here? Would he dare?

Why not?

The noise would be muffled by all the sounds in the station. If he moved fast enough, he would be halfway to the exit before anyone realized I was spilling my guts on the floor.

My uncle was standing right in front of me. He looked at Marko, then at me. "What's going on? Are you OK?"

"He's got a gun."

Uncle Harvey looked at the way we were standing, the position of Marko's arm, and his voice changed, deepened. "Let him go."

"I will," said Marko. "If you give me the letters."

"You can have whatever you want. Just let him go."

"Where are they?"

"In here." Uncle Harvey lifted his bag.

"This is what we're going to do," said Marko. "You give the bag to Tom. He'll give it to me. Then you're both going to walk away. You got that?"

"We'll do whatever you want," said Uncle Harvey. "Just don't hurt him."

"I won't."

"You'd better not."

"Don't worry, mate. We're cool. I don't want to hurt anyone. I just want those letters. Hand them over. Nice and slow."

Uncle Harvey gave the bag to me. Now I was holding one

in each hand, mine in my right and his in my left. People were pushing past us, carrying children and their own bags, and a few of them cast curious glances in our direction, but none of them stopped to see what was really happening. I heard a voice crying, "Chai! Chai!"

Marko said, "Tom, you turn round. Slowly."

I did as I was told.

I could see the gun under his jacket, the muzzle pointing directly at my chest.

"Put the bags on the floor," he said.

"Both?"

"Both."

I bent my knees and lowered both bags to the ground, then straightened up again.

"Thanks," said Marko. "Now get out of here."

I could hear Uncle Harvey's voice coming from behind me. "Don't worry. We're going."

I was watching Marko's face. I saw his eyes lift from my face and look over my shoulder, focusing on my uncle. He couldn't watch both of us at the same time, and he must have decided that I was the lesser threat. He was right, of course. But I did have one definite advantage over my uncle: I was standing next to a kid who was carrying a bucket full of tea.

I turned to face my uncle, tipped my body to one side, reached into the bucket, and grabbed the teapot. Then I whirled back again, swinging the pot at Marko's face.

*That's for Grandpa.*

If I'd been thinking straight, if I'd been less furious and upset, I'd never have done it. If Marko had happened to glance in my direction and seen what I was doing, he could have shot me before my fingers even clasped around the handle of that teapot. But I was lucky. His attention was on my uncle. He wasn't bothered about me. I guess he didn't take me seriously because I was just a kid.

Big mistake.

I don't know how much tea was in that pot, but it must have been enough to fill several cups, because it splashed all over Marko's face, covering him with scalding liquid. He screamed and clawed at his eyes with both hands, dropping his gun on the floor. All around us, people turned to stare. I could hear shouts. Someone pushed me. I stumbled. Reached down. Grabbed my uncle's bag. I didn't bother with mine—or the gun. Then I turned around and started running.

Someone was holding my arm.

I turned, expecting to see Marko, and found myself face-to-face with the kid whose tea I had just stolen.

He was shouting at me.

I couldn't understand him, but I knew what he was saying.

*Who's gonna pay for my tea?*

I yanked my arm away.

He wouldn't let go.

Behind him, I could see Marko, doubled over, one hand holding his face, the other scrabbling around on the floor for his gun. Then his fingers closed on the handle.

The kid and I struggled, me pulling and him refusing to let go.

I was screaming. He was screaming.

Suddenly he was stumbling backwards.

Uncle Harvey had shoved him away.

The kid tripped over Marko, who was just raising himself upright. They fell to the floor in a mess of arms and legs.

Now Uncle Harvey pulled the bag out of my hand and flung me forward. I didn't know which way I was going, but it didn't matter. We just had to get away from Marko.

We'd almost reached the exit when I heard someone shouting. I risked a quick glance over my shoulder. There was Marko, divided from us by the crowd, his face scarlet, his eyes murderous. He raised his hand. I could see the gun.

Would he risk a shot?

I didn't want to wait around to find out, just ducked my head and kept moving, waiting for the sound of a gunshot, the feeling of a bullet ripping into my shoulder or thudding into my back, knocking me to the floor.

Fear drove me onward. Knocking people aside. Ignoring their anger.

My uncle took us through a high doorway. A line of people were waiting for taxis. He marched straight to the front of the line.

A young, smartly dressed couple was about to climb in a yellow taxi. Uncle Harvey pushed ahead of them and took the taxi for himself.

I arrived just in time to hear the man complaining. "You cannot queue-barge like you own this place!"

"I'm in a hurry," said Uncle Harvey. "Tom, get in!"

"We are hurrying also! Please, will you return to the back of the queue."

Other people had begun shouting and gesticulating, telling Uncle Harvey to take his turn. The driver got involved too, hopping out of his seat to grab my uncle's sleeve. "You must wait. There is a queue."

"Will you take us to Mysore?" said Uncle Harvey.

The driver smiled. "Mysore is a very long way."

"If you don't want to take us . . ." My uncle looked down the line of taxis, searching for another driver. I don't know how he could be so cool. Why didn't he just shout at the driver and tell him to drive?

But his coolness seemed to do the trick, because the driver said, "Wait, sir. I will take you. But it will cost one thousand rupees."

He was probably just plucking a price out of the air, imagining that we would try to bargain him down to something more reasonable, but my uncle didn't even hesitate. "Done."

The driver could hardly believe his luck. "Get in, sirs. Please, take your seats. My car is your car."

We jumped into the back of the cab and slammed the

door. The couple stared at us open-mouthed. The driver slammed his foot on the accelerator and we were away.

Just as our taxi screeched up the road, I saw Marko emerging through the doorway. He ran to the taxis and tried to grab the first in line for himself, but the young couple wouldn't be pushed aside so easily again. The man struggled with Marko. An arm went up. Then we turned a corner and I saw nothing more.

# 18

***My uncle and I*** peered through the taxi's little rear window, scanning the streets behind us, searching for Marko. Had he escaped from that crowd? Had he found a taxi willing to take him? Would he suddenly appear in the road, raising his pistol and taking a shot at our tires?

We turned one corner, then another. He wasn't following us.

Uncle Harvey leaned forward and offered the driver an extra five hundred rupees if he could drive faster.

The driver nodded confidently. "We will be there double-quick."

Uncle Harvey flopped against the seat and grinned at me.

"You're good," he said. "I liked your move with the tea. How did you know how to do that?"

For once I didn't feel like joking around with my uncle. "He killed Grandpa," I said.

"Did he say so?"

"Yes."

"Are you sure?"

"Yes."

"He might have been lying."

"Why would he?"

"To scare you."

"No. He was telling the truth."

Uncle Harvey nodded. "It does make sense. I didn't really understand how Dad had died in his armchair. That wasn't his style."

"What are we going to do?"

"Nothing."

"Why not?"

"Because there's nothing we can do."

"We could call the police."

"They won't help. No, we'll just carry on as we'd planned. We'll get the tiger. Go home. Then we can think about Marko."

"That's it? We're just going to carry on as if nothing is different?"

"Exactly."

From the way he smiled at me, I could see there was no point arguing with Uncle Harvey. He wasn't going to change his mind. All his attention was focused on the tiger, the money, and paying off his debts. I couldn't understand it. "I know you don't want to get your legs broken. I wouldn't want to either. But what about Grandpa?"

"What about him?"

"Don't you want to get revenge? What about the honor of our family? Isn't that more important than money?"

"No." Uncle Harvey grinned. "Our family doesn't have any honor. We're just interested in money."

"That's not true."

"It is, actually. What's the point of honor if your legs are broken? If my father were here, he'd say the same thing. You didn't really know him, Tom. I did. I know what he was like. I know exactly what he would have said in this situation. Forget honor. Forget revenge. Forget Marko. Get that two million. That's why you came here and that's what you should be thinking about."

"What about—"

He interrupted me. "I'll make a deal with you, Tom. We'll find the tiger and get the money. Then we'll track down Marko. Agreed?"

"I suppose so."

"Good."

We roared out of the city and onto the Mysore road, a two-lane highway thronged with traffic. Our driver drove as if he were auditioning for Formula One, ramming his foot on the accelerator and whistling from one side of the road to the other, careening around other cars, bombing past buses and trucks, overtaking everything, never worrying about his own safety or anyone else's. He had no fear.

My uncle and I didn't talk. I was thinking about Marko. I remembered the expression in his eyes, the way he'd told me about Grandpa. I hated him. If I'd been alone in that taxi, I would have told the driver to turn around, gone back to Bangalore, and tried to find him. I wished I weren't a kid. I wished I could have come to India alone. I wished my uncle was different. Why didn't he care about honor and revenge? What was so important about money?

We'd been driving for about an hour when Uncle Harvey told the driver that we'd changed our mind about our destination. We didn't want to go to Mysore after all. Instead we were heading straight for Srirangapatna. "You don't have to worry," added Uncle Harvey. "You'll still get the same fee."

"No problem," the driver said, and rammed his foot even more enthusiastically on the accelerator, swerving into the middle of the road to overtake a bus. A truck was heading straight for us, but the driver didn't seem bothered, serenely passing first one bus, then another, before pulling back in. The truck's slipstream shook us from side to side.

To my surprise, we arrived in Srirangapatna alive. As we approached the city through some anonymous suburbs, the driver asked us where we wanted to be dropped and Uncle Harvey said, "Right here."

"You want here?"

"Yes. Here. Pull up here."

"But here is not Srirangapatna. Here is nowhere!"

"That's perfect."

The driver swerved and parked by the side of the road. We must have been on the outskirts of Srirangapatna, nowhere special, just a suburban road lined with cheap houses. I could see a shop selling satellite dishes and a café with a few old men sitting outside at flimsy wooden tables. Traffic roared past, heading into the city center. No one else was stopping here.

Uncle Harvey counted out fifteen hundred rupees, as agreed.

The driver took the money, then asked, "One tip?"

"You'd be lucky."

"I am very lucky," said the driver with a cheeky grin, and I couldn't help liking him, even if he was a suicidal maniac. My uncle must have liked him too, because he handed over another grubby bill. The driver thanked him and jumped back into his car. He executed a nifty U-turn, narrowly missing a bus coming the other way, and accelerated back toward Bangalore.

Once he'd disappeared down the road in a cloud of dust, my uncle said, "Now let's find another taxi."

"Why didn't we just keep that one?"

"Taxis are easy to trace. I don't want to leave a trail for Marko. Or J.J. Or anyone else who might be following us. Shall we walk into town? I think it must be this way."

My uncle led the way along the wonky pavement. The houses looked as if they'd been recently bombed or experienced an earthquake. Cracks shimmied up the walls, and some of the windows had no glass. Two nervous dogs skittered out of our way. A man hurried across the street and smiled at us. "You want a Tipu guide?"

"No, thank you," replied my uncle.

"I am all-knowing Tipu Sultan. You will come with me and see the remains of his fort and palace?"

I couldn't see any ruins and ancient monuments, let alone other tourists, so I couldn't imagine this guy was a real guide. If he wanted to take people around the fort and the palace, wouldn't he be waiting there, meeting them as they came off their coaches? Why would he be out here in the suburbs?

My uncle didn't bother asking any of these questions. "We don't need a guide," he said. "We just need a taxi."

"Come this way. Follow me. I will guide you for taxi."

I wouldn't have followed some random guy who came up to me in the street, but my uncle seemed perfectly happy to trust him, so we let the guide lead us around the corner to a shady spot where a yellow auto-rickshaw was parked by the side of the road. I could see a pair of bare feet poking out of the window; the driver must have been having a nap inside his vehicle. Our guide whistled. The driver sat up and poked his head out. To my surprise, he was just a kid. He looked about the same age as me, and maybe a year or two younger. I'm thin, but this guy was so skinny that his bones would have snapped in a strong breeze. "You want one taxi?" he called to us. "I am ready and available for hire! Please to come aboard!"

My uncle gave a few rupees to our guide, who bowed his head gratefully. "Thank you so much, sir. If you change your mind and wish for full Tipu tour, you will please come to find me. I have expert knowledge of all relevant historical monuments."

The kid was already ushering us eagerly toward his rickshaw. "Welcome in my taxi," he said. "Please, you will go where? To the Tipu Palace? The gardens? You will have one stop for restaurant? You are hungry? You are thirsty? You want to buy good jewels? I know best shop."

"Calm down, kid. We don't want to buy anything." Uncle Harvey's phone had a map. A flashing blue dot showed our current position. He pointed to where we wanted to go. "Can you take us here?"

"No problem, I will take you anywhere, you just tell me where." The kid peered at the tiny screen. "What is the name of this place?"

"I don't know."

"You do not know where you are going?"

"We want to head north. Somewhere around here," said my uncle, gesturing vaguely again at the tiny map on the tiny screen of his tiny phone.

Unsurprisingly, the kid was confused. "Round there means round where?"

"Don't worry about that," said Uncle Harvey. "We'll know when we get there."

"No problem. We will find it. If you please to come aboard."

We clambered inside his rickshaw, which wobbled under our weight. A long crack ran across the entire length of the windshield. Stuffing wisped through slashes in the seats.

There were no doors and no seat belts, just a rail to hang on to. It looked decrepit and dangerous and entirely fantastic. I wanted to drive it myself. Later I'd have to ask our driver if I could give it a shot.

Once the motor was puttering away and the rickshaw was ready to go, the kid turned around and grinned at us. "You are comfy?"

"Yes, thanks," said my uncle.

"The cushion is good?"

I nodded. "Perfect."

"Good. My name is Suresh."

He waited for a moment as if he was expecting us to tell him our names in exchange, but my uncle just said, "Could you switch on the meter?"

"Meter no working," said Suresh.

"Oh, yeah. I've heard that one before."

"It is true, sir. But not a problem. You will pay what you want."

"No, thanks," said my uncle. He swung one leg out of the rickshaw. "If you won't switch on your meter, we'll find another cab."

"But I am telling you already, the meter is not working!"

"Yeah, yeah, yeah. Come on, Tom. We're outta here."

"Wait a minute." I turned to the kid. "What did you mean, we'd pay what we wanted? How would that work?"

"Like I say, you pay what you want. You like my service, you give me good money. You no like, you no pay."

"You mean, we'd get a free ride?"

"Yes! India is a free country. Free economy. Free enterprise. You pay what you want."

"That's crazy," said Uncle Harvey. "What if you drive us for the whole day and go a hundred miles, but we only give you ten rupees?"

"It is for you to choose. I am telling you, sir, this is the best system."

"Fine. If that's how you want to play it, that's how we'll play it." My uncle shifted himself back into the cab. "It sounds insane to me, but it's your cab. You can do what you like."

"Thank you, sir."

Suresh revved the throttle. The rickshaw jerked forward, spluttered down the road, and swept us into the lines of traffic toward our tiger.

# 19

***We soon left the town*** behind and drove through the countryside, heading north. Palm trees sprang out of the earth like big hands gesturing at the sky. White bullocks pulled wooden plows through the fields. We passed a man on a horse, clip-clopping slowly up the road, and I had a vision of Horatio Trelawney riding this way more than two hundred years ago, the sounds of the battle still ringing in his ears.

I turned to my uncle. "Can I see the letter?"

"Which letter?"

"The last one. The one about the hill. I'd like to check what Horatio said."

"Good idea." He unzipped his bag, pulled out the treasure box, and unfolded the final letter so we could both read it.

*I might have ridden twenty, or I might have ridden thirty miles, it was not easy to know. The landscape was so hilly and the roads so rough that any accurate figure is beyond me.*

Horatio had left only the vaguest directions for us to follow: head north for something between twenty and thirty miles. Stop when you come to a small hill topped with a rickety stone shrine. Then climb to the top.

*To my astonishment, I found a small shrine on the top of the hill.*

We just had to hope it was still there.

Our rickshaw whizzed us through a village of small houses with straw roofs. Suresh blasted his horn, scattering children and chickens, then the dust whirled and they were gone.

The road went on and on. My throat was dry. My butt ached. Only a finger-thin cushion lay between me and the hard seat, and the uneven surface bounced us about mercilessly.

My hands hurt too. I had to cling on to the metal struts or I would have been thrown out of the rickshaw whenever we went over a bump.

But I couldn't stop grinning.

Driving in a funny little vehicle halfway between a van and a scooter, heading into a strange landscape, baked by the sun, hunting for treasure—what could be better than this?

The same sights repeated again and again, fields and trees and oxen and cyclists, the monotony broken only by the occasional car careening down the road toward us, furiously hooting its horn, ordering us out of its way, then roaring past and leaving our little rickshaw in a cloud of dust. There was only one law on these roads: biggest is best.

Uncle Harvey had been looking over Suresh's shoulder, keeping an eye on the odometer, and suddenly announced, "We've gone eighteen miles. It should be soon."

Horatio had taken an entire morning to ride this route on his horse. Even in our battered, spluttering three-wheeled rickshaw, we'd done the same journey in less than an hour.

We took a side each, Uncle Harvey on the left and me on the right, and peered at the landscape.

Five minutes passed. Then another five. The road curved. And I saw what we were looking for.

I nudged my uncle. "That's it." I spoke in a low voice, not wanting Suresh to hear me. "Look. Do you see?"

Uncle Harvey crowded over to my side of the rickshaw and peered out of the open doorway. Together we stared at the hill. It was exactly as Horatio had described, a small, steep mound springing straight out of the dusty plain.

Now we just had to climb up there, find the hole in the ground, dig up the tiger—and we'd be rich.

Uncle Harvey waited for us to come right up to the hill, then tapped Suresh on his shoulder. "We'll stop here, please."

"Here, sir?" shouted Suresh.

"Yes. Here."

We glided to a standstill by the side of the road.

Uncle Harvey and I stepped out. The heat was astonishing. While the rickshaw was moving, a breeze had been cooling us down, but stepping out of it onto the road was like putting your head in an oven.

Suresh watched us curiously. He asked, "You will go where?"

"Up there." I pointed to the top of the hill.

"Why?"

I wasn't sure how to answer, but luckily Uncle Harvey took over. "We want to see the view. Will you wait for us here, please? We won't be long."

"You will leave your bag?" asked Suresh. "Is safe with me."

"That's not a bad idea," said Uncle Harvey. He pulled a few valuables out of the bag, zipped it up, and dumped it on the back seat. "You're not going to steal it, are you?"

"No, sir!" Suresh looked shocked at the very idea. "I am your driver, not a thief! I will keep it safe for you."

"Just checking. See you later."

I thought about my bag, now in Marko's possession. What was in there? Anything I needed? Clothes. Shoes. Two books. The charger for my phone. Toothbrush, toothpaste. The only thing I'd actually miss was my favorite T-shirt, a nice blue one with a picture of a skull on it. For a horrible moment, I thought he might steal it for himself, but then I realized it would be much too small for him. I was glad about that. There was something really gross about the thought of Marko wearing my best T-shirt.

As we walked away from the road, Suresh squatted in the shade cast by his rickshaw and stared at us. I could imagine the questions going through his mind. What were we doing? Why would anyone get out of a nice comfortable rickshaw in the middle of nowhere and start climbing a hill at the hottest time of day?

*You just wait. We'll be back with two million dollars.*

Obviously I didn't say that. I just grinned at him and kept walking.

Uncle Harvey set a brisk pace. His legs were longer than mine and I soon dropped behind. I had to climb the hill staring at his back, watching the first prickles of sweat appear under his armpits, then widen into puddles.

The sunlight beat down on my face. I could hear my mom's voice. *Where's your hat? What about sunblock? Haven't you heard of skin cancer?* Yadda, yadda, yadda. The same old stuff that moms have to say.

Actually, if she *had* said all that stuff, she would have been right. I really needed a hat. And some sunblock. And, more than anything, water. The sun was slicing through my skull like a blowtorch, and soon I was sweating almost as much as my uncle.

Forget it. We were almost at the top. Just a few more minutes. Then the agony would be over. A million dollars would soon make up for a bit of sunburn.

Up we went, side by side, silent, neither of us wanting to waste our breath on conversation.

Up and up and up.

Up and up and up.

We stumbled to the top of the hill, panting and sweat-sodden, and emerged on the summit, and found . . .

# 20

***. . . nothing.***

The hilltop was flat and empty. There wasn't the slightest sign that a shrine had ever been built here. Where had it gone?

What had happened in the past two hundred years?

According to Horatio's letter, his shrine hadn't been much. From his description, I'd imagined nothing more than a hole in the ground. But I couldn't even see a hole up here.

How would we find it again? How could we ever discover where it had been? Would we have to dig up this entire hill for ourselves?

We didn't even have a spade.

"I guess we climbed the wrong hill," said my uncle.

"It might be the right one." I was trying to stay positive. "It fits Horatio's description."

"Yes, but so do they all."

"What do you mean, 'they all'?"

"Look."

Until that moment, all my attention had been fixed on the summit where we were standing, searching for the remnants of a well, a spring, a deep, dark hole that might have hidden a tiger for two hundred years. Now I looked around us.

From the height of this hill, I could see the undulating landscape stretching in every direction. There must have been forty more hills almost identical to ours, and those were only the ones that we could see. If we drove up the road, we'd probably find hundreds more, valley after valley giving way to summit after summit, every one exactly as Horatio had described.

I was daunted for a moment. I don't mind admitting that. I had a few seconds of worry: Had we messed up? Should we have stayed at home? Was this whole thing a waste of time? What if the letters were forgeries? What if the whole thing was a trick dreamed up by Grandpa to steal a rich man's money? Had we been stupid enough to fall for one of Grandpa's cons?

Then I told myself not to be such a loser. We had a whole week here in India. That was long enough to climb every hill for miles around. And if it was a con, who cared? Being here was still a lot more interesting than being with my family or going back to school.

I turned to my uncle. "Shall we try the next one?"

"Sure. Race you to the bottom."

# 21

**We drove north,** parked the rickshaw, said goodbye to Suresh again, and climbed another hill. By the time we got to the top, I was drenched in sweat. It wasn't the one we were looking for. We walked down, drove on, got out, climbed the next. Nothing. Then one more. Nothing. And yet another. Nothing there, either.

Suresh must have thought we were insane, but he never questioned what we were doing, just did as we asked and drove us down the road till we told him to stop again, then sat in the shade of a tree and watched us struggle up yet another rock-strewn gradient.

That hill, the sixth of them, was the most difficult so far. I don't know if the slope was actually steeper or if I was just getting tired, but it was a real struggle to get to the top. And a bitter disappointment to find it empty. There was nothing there at all. Not even a tree. Just a few windswept shrubs, none of them hiding a hole or a pile of rocks.

I stood beside my uncle, staring at the sunbaked view.

The landscape seemed to stretch forever: hills and shrubs and trees and a single road zigzagging along the valley.

"Ready for one more?" said Uncle Harvey.

"Sure."

After six hills, neither of us had the energy for running. We trudged slowly back down to the bottom and found Suresh sitting under the shade of a tree. He held up a metal flask. "You want one drink?"

"Yes, please." I reached for the flask.

To my surprise, Uncle Harvey stopped me. "You'd better not. You can't drink the water in India unless you know exactly where it's come from."

"I'm about to die of thirst!"

"I'll buy you a bottle."

"Oh, yeah?" I gestured at the empty plains surrounding us. "Where?"

Uncle Harvey turned to Suresh. "Is there a shop round here? Or a restaurant?"

"You want tiffin stop?"

"Indeed we do," said Uncle Harvey. "Do you know anywhere nice?"

"I know very good place."

"Is it owned by one of your relatives? Do you get a commission for taking us there?"

"No, sir! Just good food. Please to come aboard and we will go."

Tiffin was an Indian word for a meal. That's what my uncle told me. He'd been to India many times before and knew all the lingo.

We got back in the rickshaw and headed north.

We'd stop for a quick lunch, Uncle Harvey said, then carry on searching for the rest of the afternoon, returning to Srirangapatna in time to find a hotel before nightfall. Tomorrow we would continue our search.

"What if we haven't found the tiger by the end of the week?" I asked. "Will we stay another week?"

"You've got to go back to the States."

"I don't care."

"I do."

"What about you? Will you stay here on your own?"

"I can't go home without the money to pay my debts," said Uncle Harvey. "I had been planning to spend this week trying to gather together a hundred grand, but I'm here instead. If I don't get my hands on some cash, I might have to stay here for the rest of my life. Which wouldn't be too bad, actually. I love India. I could join an ashram and spend my days meditating."

"What's an ashram?"

As we drove on, Uncle Harvey told me about Hinduism and Buddhism and all the different gods and religions that you find in India. He told me about sadhus, the holy men who have no money and no possessions, just their clothes, their sandals, and a walking stick. We would see one soon, he said. I would recognize them by their shaved heads. He might become one of them himself, he suggested, if he couldn't find the money to pay off his debts: he would shave his head, swap his clothes for a yellow robe, and spend the rest of his life walking around India, begging for food and coins. To my surprise, he seemed quite keen on the idea.

When we'd been driving for fifteen or twenty minutes, Suresh turned off the main road and rattled us up a dusty lane that soon led to what looked like a small town. Shacks lined the roadside and some kind of big building stood on the top of the nearest hill, looking down on us. It could have been a castle or just more houses, sheltering behind a high wall, protecting the inhabitants from attack. Chickens clucked and squabbled out of our way. A naked toddler giggled at us as if we were clowns putting on a show just for him.

We pulled up at a small restaurant. Wooden tables and plastic chairs were laid out under a wide awning, providing shade from the hot sun. The place wasn't exactly buzzing. An Indian family was sitting at one of the tables, the parents and three kids sharing a big spread, and a female backpacker was at another, a hippie in a pink T-shirt and baggy blue trousers. She glanced at us for a moment, then went back to her book. I smelled spices from the kitchen and realized how hungry I was.

We sat by the door. Suresh went to sit alone at a different table. I felt bad. Why didn't he join us? Shouldn't we ask him over? Actually, maybe better not. He might ask too many awkward questions. He'd obviously been interested in what we were doing, but he'd kept his curiosity to himself, and it would be best if that didn't change. Marko might be right behind us, and we didn't want him to be able to discover what we were doing.

"What do you want to eat?" asked Uncle Harvey.

I didn't have to think about it. I had the same whenever we went out for Indian or if Dad got takeout on a night when Mom was too tired to cook. "Lamb rogan josh, pilau rice, and naan bread, please. And some mango chutney."

"You won't get that here."

"Why not? We're in India, aren't we?"

"All those dishes are from the north. We're in the south. It's all masala dosas and idli sambas."

"It's what?"

"You've never had a masala dosa?"

"No."

"You're going to enjoy this." He looked around for a waiter. Then he said, "Maybe we should ask her to join us."

I thought I must have misheard "her" for "him," but when Uncle Harvey sprang to his feet and loped across the restaurant, I realized he had forgotten our driver. All his attention had been taken up by that backpacker with baggy pants and a silver ring through her nose. A few moments later, he was beckoning me over. He'd managed to convince the woman that we should join her table.

Did he think she'd be useful to us? Did he hope she could help us find the tiger?

No. He just liked her.

My uncle could sometimes be a real idiot.

The hippie stood up and shook my hand. Her name was Tanya, she said, and she was from Israel. My uncle told her our names, explained where we were from, and waved the waiter over to order a round of mango lassies. "You're going to love this," he said to me. Then he turned back to the hippie. "Tom's never been to India before. This is his first time."

"Do you like it?" she asked in her heavy accent.

"So far."

"Where have you been?"

"Only Bengaluru and here."

"Why do you come here? To see the temple?"

"We're here because, um . . ." I looked at my uncle for help.

"My nephew is doing a school project on Tipu Sultan and the Duke of Wellington. We've come on a research trip. We're visiting all the places associated with Tipu and the battlefield where Wellington finally defeated him."

"Really? You've brought him all the way to India for school? That's so wonderful. You must be his favorite uncle!"

"I am. But I'm also his only uncle, so there's not much competition." Uncle Harvey grinned and the girl laughed. Soon they were chatting away like old friends. She lived in Tel Aviv, she told us, but she loved traveling around the world, seeing how different people lived. She and my uncle discussed the different places that they'd been in India, comparing their experiences. I listened but didn't say much, having decided that my only possible role was stopping my uncle from saying anything too stupid, anything that might give away clues to our real reason for being here. I didn't think Tanya was a spy or a friend of Marko's. Even he wouldn't be able to get someone here so quickly. But I still thought it would be best if she didn't know too much about us.

A mango lassi, I can tell you now, is a sweet, yogurty drink. As for a masala dosa, that turned out to be a large crispy pancake, rolled up and curled around a lump of vegetable curry studded with peas, potatoes, and tiny peppercorns. The only cutlery was a teaspoon in the spicy brown sauce that came with it. Uncle Harvey showed me how to tear off a chunk of the pancake with my fingers, wrap it around the vegetables, and dip it in the sauce.

"Only use your right hand," he said, winking at Tanya. "Indians keep their left hand for wiping their bum. If they see you eating with your left hand, they won't come anywhere near you."

Tanya said, "What do you think of the food, Tom? Do you like it?"

"It's great," I said. And it was: although it tasted nothing like any curry that I'd ever tasted before, the pancake was crispy and delicious, and the sauce had a great spicy taste that was milder and more interesting than curries at home.

"Most of the Indian restaurants in the U.S. serve north Indian food," said my uncle. "Their food is nice enough, but

I prefer south Indian. You should sample as much as you can when you're here. You just have to be prepared for the occasional dose of amoebic dysentery."

"Oh, I was so sick last week!" said Tanya.

"What happened?"

"It was my own stupid fault. I ate an ice cream. Everyone tells you, never eat ice cream. Whatever you do, never eat ice cream in India, you will be sick immediately. That's what they say, right? But I was in a nice place, and it was clean, and I thought, *Why not?* So I spent the next twenty-four hours sitting on the john."

"Sitting?" My uncle shook his head. "You've got nothing to complain about!"

"What do you mean?"

"At least it wasn't coming out from both ends at the same time."

"Oh, that's terrible." Tanya winced.

"Would you mind?" I said. "I'm trying to eat."

Neither of them took any notice. I'm not sure Uncle Harvey even heard me. All his attention was focused on the girl. He leaned across the table and said in a low tone, "Have you ever been on a bus with dysentery?"

"That's the worst," she replied. "I took this bus once from Srinagar to Delhi, and I had to spend the whole journey locked in the tiny toilet at the back . . ."

And so it went on, Uncle Harvey and his new best friend trying to outdo each other with their tales of disgusting illnesses. I'm not squeamish, but all their talk about diarrhea didn't do my food any favors. Eventually I couldn't take it anymore. I picked up my plate and walked away. Rather than returning to our original table, I joined Suresh. He looked up, smiling. "You are ready for leaving?"

"I wish I could say yes, but we might have to wait for Uncle Harvey to pick up that girl first."

"We must wait to get what?"

"Nothing. I'm just joking. I should think we'll go soon, yes. We want to climb a few more hills before it gets dark."

"If you don't mind me asking, why are you doing this?"

"I can't explain. I'm sorry."

"No problem." Suresh shrugged his shoulders. "I am only driver, there is no need to tell me."

I said, "Can I sit down here?"

"Please, no problem."

I sat opposite him. We sat there awkwardly for a moment, then he broke the silence. "You are from which country?"

"The U.S.," I said.

"Ah, United States! You love football?"

"Not really. I prefer baseball."

"Yankees?"

"No, Red Sox."

"Oh, yes. Win World Series."

"Hey, tell me something. Is this your village? Do you live here?"

"No, no. This is not my village."

"But you've been here before?"

"Yes."

"Why?"

"This is the home of one temple. You see? Here, come, look."

He pointed at the hill behind us. The awning that stretched above our heads had obscured my view of what I had thought was a castle.

In his halting English, Suresh explained that he had been to the temple several times with his mother, because she was very sick.

"What's wrong with her?" I asked.

He said the word for her illness in his own language. Seeing it meant nothing to me, he described the symptoms. I couldn't be sure, but it sounded to me like cancer. He explained that his family came here to seek help for her illness, bringing offerings for the god of this temple.

"Is she getting any better?"

"Not yet," said Suresh. "But she will soon."

"How do you know?"

"Because the temple god, he will help us. Excuse me, sir. There is one thing I must ask. It is possible for me to go there?"

"To the temple?"

"Yes. I wish to make one offering."

"How long will it take?"

"Only ten or maybe twenty minutes."

"I don't see why not."

I looked across the restaurant. Tanya had rolled back her sleeve to expose a tattoo on her forearm, and my uncle was leaning across the table to get a better look. I turned back to Suresh. "Actually, can I come with you?"

# 22

***At the bottom of the steps,*** two men were standing beside a chair lashed to two long wooden poles. They smiled and beckoned, pointing at their strange contraption, and I realized they were offering to lug me to the top.

I said, "How far is it?"

"Three hundred steps," replied Suresh. "You are happy for walking?"

"No problem."

I'd just walked up six hills. I didn't mind three hundred stone steps.

We continued past the guys with the chair-lift and plodded up the steps side by side, talking all the way. Suresh told me more about his life. He had three sisters and a brother, all younger than him. Their dad had died in a car accident the year before last. That was why he had to drive his taxi. The family needed money for food, rent, and his mother's medicines, and no one else was old enough to work.

"How old are you?"

"I am twelve years."

"Don't you have to go to school?"

"I have not time. If I earn good money, my brother will go to the school, but not me."

That's cool, I almost said, but managed to stop myself before the words left my mouth. Skipping school would be cool, and so would driving a rickshaw, but I was sure Suresh couldn't see many advantages to having a dead dad and a sick mother.

I told him about myself and my own life: my school, the golf cart, and getting grounded, which made me miss out on an overnight sailing trip with my friend Finn, which had annoyed me more than anything else till Grandpa's lunch.

Suresh pointed out the halfway mark, an old tree covered in red paint. Only a hundred and fifty steps to go.

Above, awaiting us, I could see the high walls enclosing the temple, and the decorations on the structure itself, hundreds of statues standing in lines, all the way up to the lopped-off triangle at its peak. As we came closer, I could see that the statues were figures, but I couldn't make out whether they were gods, people, or animals.

Beggars were sitting on the stairs, holding out their hands, asking for coins. One was blind, his eyes milky-white, his hand reaching in my direction, his grubby fingers fluttering through the air. Another had no legs, the stumps sticking out of her frayed trousers, angled on the ground like two bits of wood. "Money," she moaned. "Please, sir, give me money."

I wished I could help, but I didn't have any cash. I muttered an apology and hurried after Suresh. Uncle Harvey would have been proud of me. Was he really right? Wouldn't it be better to give money to one or two beggars, even if you couldn't pay them all? You're never going to solve everyone's problems, but shouldn't you help one or two if you could? As we went past more and more beggars, some missing limbs, others blind or deformed, I felt worse and worse about having nothing to give them. Once we found the tiger and sold it, I'd come back here and hand out some money, sharing my good fortune with these beggars.

At the top of the steps, we came to a high gate, the entrance to the temple.

"You must take off your shoes," said Suresh.

"Why?"

"This is the rule."

We placed our shoes on a wooden rack. Alongside the rows of other people's grubby leather sandals and plastic flip-flops, my sneakers looked very white, clean, and modern.

"Will anyone take them?" I asked Suresh.

"No. This is temple. There is no stealing."

I hoped he was right. I didn't want to go home barefoot.

We walked under another doorway and into a large, square courtyard with gates on all four sides leading to different parts of the temple. Hundreds of people were milling around. Most of them were staring at me. That's what it felt like, anyway. Maybe they didn't get many foreigners here, or especially foreign kids. I saw some of the sadhus that Uncle Harvey had told me about. Old men in yellow or white robes, their heads shaved, sitting cross-legged on the floor, chatting and laughing.

There were statues everywhere: attached to the walls, carved on the pillars, clinging to the tower, looking down on us. There might have been thousands of them, all different shapes and sizes. As far as I could tell, they were all supposed to be human, or semi-human. Some had the heads of animals. Many more had extra arms and legs popping out of their bodies, waggling and waving. A few were white, but most of them had been painted the most garish colors, bright pinks and greens and yellows and blues, as if they'd put on their craziest clothes for a fancy-dress party.

I followed Suresh across the courtyard and through another gateway. A man blocked our way, wearing nothing but a little strap of white cloth around his middle. He grinned toothlessly at me and stretched out his hand, begging for money. I dodged past and sprinted after Suresh.

We came to a square pool with steps leading down to the murky water. Men stood at one end, women at the other, splashing water over themselves. The women went in fully clothed, their saris clinging to their skin, while the men wore nothing more than underpants. The pool was big enough, and must have been deep enough, but no one was actually swimming.

A couple of monkeys were playing in the trees. One of them jumped down and scampered across the courtyard, heading for a pile of bags. His little head turned frantically from side to side, checking to see if he had been noticed. He slid his paw inside one of the bags and yanked out a banana.

An old man waddled out of the pool, water dripping down his legs, shouting and waving his arms, but the monkey had already raced away and now was high above him, squatting on a branch, peeling the banana. He ate the whole thing and, as if he couldn't resist one final insult, tossed the peel into the pool.

I would have been happy to watch the monkeys for hours, but Suresh was already walking across the courtyard to a doorway guarded by four men. They were dressed in simple white uniforms and carrying thick bamboo poles, about the length of their arms. They watched us carefully as we went past, as if they were searching for weaponry or evil intent.

One of the guards tried to stop me, but Suresh came back and spoke to him in their own language, and I was allowed inside.

Moving from the brightness of the sunlit courtyard to the gloom of the temple, I was blinded for a few seconds, but my eyes soon adjusted and I could see we were walking through a large, square room. The walls were covered in carvings and several women were sitting on the floor, chopping fruit and putting the pieces in wooden bowls. Suresh handed a few coins to one of the women and took two bowls. He gave one to me.

"For the gods," he said.

"The gods like fruit?"

"The gods must eat. Come, we will find them."

The fruit looked like a cross between a mango and a melon, and smelled delicious. I wanted to try some. Would the gods mind if I nibbled their dinner?

I felt bad Suresh had bought my fruit. When I got my hands on some money, I'd have to pay him back.

We came to an elephant. He was chained to a thick pillar. Bright colors had been painted over his tough gray skin. He was standing so still that I thought he must be an amazingly realistic statue, then he turned to look at us, blinked his big sad eyes, and stretched out his trunk, the soft end twitching and reaching for our hands.

Next we passed a man standing on one leg. His other leg was bent back and tucked into his groin. I've tried standing on one leg for as long as possible and I can usually last a couple of minutes, but this guy was rock solid. He didn't even wobble.

We went through another door and crossed a room paneled with pale wood, then around a dark corridor and under an archway, and came to the heart of the temple, the innermost room, a quiet place bathed by candlelight and sweet incense. Only one other person was in there, an old bald man who was sitting cross-legged on the floor. I didn't know if he was a priest or a worshiper or some kind of guard, but he gave us a big grin and clasped his palms in front of his chest. Suresh made the same gesture back again.

"Is namaste," he explained to me in a whisper.

"Namaste?"

"Yes. You try."

I placed my palms together as if I was praying and bowed my head.

The bald guy grinned and made the same gesture back to me.

"Good," said Suresh.

We turned to face the heart of the temple, a black rock glistening with oil or water, surrounded by garlands of flowers and thirty little wooden bowls filled with an offering of milk, honey, sliced mango, or peeled and chopped bananas.

Candle smoke trailed upward, curling and twisting past more orange and yellow flowers hanging from jutting-out rocks, past more statues, past more carvings of cross-legged men with animal heads and dancing women with four arms and four legs, and up toward the top of the temple, where a small hole let in a thin shaft of blinding sunlight.

As my eyes adjusted to the light, I noticed hundreds of niches carved into the walls. Some were filled with yet more flickering candles or little wooden bowls of offerings. Others held statues of muscular men and curvaceous women and impossible gods with plump bellies and writhing arms.

In the middle of the room there appeared to be a hole in the ground, covered with a few old bricks and some pieces of timber. More candles sat there and more bowls, too, filled with fruit.

"Come," said Suresh.

I pointed at the hole. "What's that?"

"For the god," he said. "For eating."

"No, not the bowls. That hole. What's down there?"

"It is the home of the god."

"He lives down there?"

"It is his home. Here, come. You must put that down."

He went forward and placed his bowl on the timber, then gestured for me to do the same.

I placed my bowl on the ground.

"Now, pray."

Suresh kneeled, clasped his hands together, and closed his eyes.

I'm not used to praying. I don't usually go to church. I wasn't even sure what to do. So I just copied Suresh, kneeling like him, putting my hands together, and closing my eyes. I felt silly. I thought everyone would be looking at me, and I opened my eyes a couple of times to check, but no one seemed to be at all interested in what I was doing. I closed my eyes again and wondered what to pray for. I probably should have prayed for Suresh's mom, but I'd never even met her, so that would have felt strange. I really wanted to pray that something bad happened to Marko, but I thought gods probably didn't like those sorts of prayers. So I prayed for Uncle Harvey's legs instead. I prayed that we'd find the tiger and sell it for a load of money so he could pay off his debts. I felt a little guilty, praying for money, so I added a promise of my own. *If we do get the money,* I said to myself, *I'll give some of it away. Some will go to Suresh for his mom. And some will go to the beggars that I keep seeing in the street.* Of course I'd keep some for myself too. I wanted a new bike and a new computer. But I wouldn't keep it all for myself.

I couldn't imagine anyone was listening to me, but if they were, that was my promise, and that was my prayer.

I half opened my eyes and snuck a look at Suresh. He was still kneeling, eyes tight shut, his lips moving. I didn't want to disturb him, but I was beginning to feel uncomfortable. I wasn't used to kneeling for such a long time. Trying not to make any noise, I shifted my legs, sat down fully, and looked around. I stared at the hole in the ground. It was like something from a movie: I could imagine an ogre or a troll sneaking up and snuffling up all the fruit in the wooden bowls.

Wait a minute. A hole in the ground. A shrine. Could it be . . . ?

Why not?

The more I thought about it, the more sense it made.

I waited for Suresh to open his eyes. Then I pointed at the hole. "Does the god ever come out of there?"

"For special moments only."

"Like when?"

"I don't know."

"When was the last time?"

"I don't know."

"You've never seen him?"

"No."

"Have you ever been down the hole?"

"No!" Suresh laughed, his eyes wide, as if I'd suggested something disgusting.

"So no one goes down there?"

"No one."

"Never?"

"Never."

*Hmm. Interesting.*

The god lived in the hole. No one went down there. No one knew what you might find down there. Which meant that if something had been down there for a couple hundred years, no one would know anything about it.

# 23

**I still had Horatio's letter** in my pocket. Making an excuse to Suresh, I moved to the back of the room and stood under a candle, using its light to read a few lines.

*To my astonishment, I found a small shrine on the top of the hill. Someone had indeed been here before me. India is full of such places. The Hindoos have the strangest love of bizarre gods.*

*This pagan shrine was no more than a few golden bricks built around a hole in the ground. A dried-up well, perhaps, or a shelter from the sun, over which some Hindoo had placed this shrine and come to worship one of his strange gods.*

*I had already wrapped my tiger in my second-best shirt. Now I pushed aside the bricks and lowered myself into the hole.*

*I found a place there to hide the tiger. No one will find him. No one but you, my sweet wife.*

This was it, I thought. It had to be. When my great-etc.-grandfather parked his horse at the bottom of the hill, there hadn't been a line of steps leading to the top, let alone a temple full of pilgrims and statues, but things change a lot in two hundred years. This was the hole. This was the shrine. And if I was lucky, the tiger would still be down there, just where Horatio put it.

I looked at the statues on the walls and the bowls around the altars and the people in here with me, the pilgrims, the priests, whoever they were, and tried to imagine how I was going to get down that hole. Obviously I couldn't just climb down there. How could I distract their attention for long enough to pull the bricks and timbers aside, then slither into the hole, carrying a flashlight or a candle, find the tiger, and bring it out again?

I should go back to the restaurant and talk to Uncle Harvey. He'd know what to do.

Of course it would be much better to get the tiger without his help.

But how could I do that?

I could wait till I was the only person in the temple. They'd have to shut it up at night. I could hide somewhere. A cupboard. A bathroom. Then I could sneak out once the temple was empty and grab the tiger.

But I was the only white guy in the place. I stood out a mile off. How was I supposed to hide?

"Mister Tom?"

Suresh was standing before me. He'd brought a friend over, a guy who was barely taller than me but must have been twenty or thirty years older. He was bare-chested and wore nothing but a white cloth wrapped around his waist like a skirt. A piece of string ran diagonally across his chest. Some dirt was dabbed on his forehead. What did it mean?

"This is Ram," said Suresh. "He is one chief priest here. You have questions, he will answer."

"Hello, Mister Tom," said Ram.

"Hi. Nice to meet you." I smiled in a way that I hoped made me look like a goofy tourist who hardly knew how he had gotten here, not a thief who was trying to work out how to steal the temple's most precious possession. "You work here, right?"

"I work here, yes. Live here also."

"Really? Where do you sleep?"

"In the temple."

"You have a room? A bedroom?"

"Yes. I share with other priests. All in one room."

"Wow. That sounds intense. India is a very spiritual country."

"No, no, India is like every other country. We have spiritual people, we have not-spiritual people. It is the same in your country, I am so sure."

"I don't think so. It's quite different where I'm from."

"It is different here," Ram said, waving his hand at the walls of the temple, the candles, the fruit, the statues. "But the same here." He pressed his hand to his chest.

Really? Was that true? I couldn't imagine any connection between this place and the religion that I knew, the religion of the vicar at Grandpa's funeral, the music crackling out of the speakers, the rain beating down on the old gravestones. But I didn't say so. I nodded and said he was probably right, we're all the same deep down.

"That is precisely correct!" Ram beamed. "We are all the same deep down!"

I don't know if he wanted to practice his English or was just naturally chatty, but Ram was eager to talk, and I was happy to carry on the conversation, because it gave me a good opportunity to learn about the temple. He told me everything that I wanted to know. The temple had been here for about a hundred years. Before that, a small shrine had sat on the top of the hill, a place where the local farmers and villagers would come to make offerings to their god, the one who lived in this hole. The gates were never locked, he told me, but were constantly guarded. There were always men on the door, checking who came in and out, and at least one priest stayed in this inner sanctum at all times, making sure the flames kept burning and the bowls of offerings were full. There were thieves here, he said, who would sneak into this room and steal the bananas, the melons, the coconut milk.

"That's terrible," I said. "What kind of people would come in here and steal the food?"

"Not people," replied Ram. "Monkeys."

"Oh, yes. I saw them by the pool. Can they get in here?"

"They want to. They smell the fruit. That is why we must have guards."

A monkey! That would be perfect. I could train it to sneak into that hole while no one was looking and steal the tiger.

No, that wouldn't work. Training a monkey would take months.

If anyone was going to grab the tiger, it would have to be me.

I was the monkey.

# 24

**Ram was called away** to perform some priestly duties, so we shook hands and each said it had been a pleasure to meet the other. He was probably just being polite, but for me, it really had been a pleasure. I liked him a lot. I even felt a little bad about grilling him for information. I began to wish I could have been here as a normal traveler, a tourist, the person that I was pretending to be, just a kid from Connecticut who had come to India on vacation.

Oh, well. Ram didn't even know the tiger existed, so he wouldn't miss it.

Ram didn't come back, but a second priest arrived a minute later carrying a shiny metal cup, which he handed to me with a smile.

The metal felt cold against my fingers. The cup was filled with a white frothy liquid. Tiny green seeds floated on the surface.

I looked at Suresh. "What is this?"

"One drink," he replied.

"But what's in it? I don't want to drink it if I don't know what it is."

"Yes, no problem. You must drink."

I took a cautious sniff.

It smelled sweet.

They're priests. Of course they wouldn't poison me.

Hoping I was right, I took a tentative sip. The white liquid was thick, cool, milky, and delicious. It tasted even better than the mango lassi I'd had in the restaurant.

I offered the cup to Suresh. "You want some?"

"No. Special for you."

"What's so special about me?"

"You are visitor. Please to drink."

I drained the cup in three or four long gulps, handed it back to the priest, and thanked him. He took the cup away with a smile, sat cross-legged on the floor, and chatted to the other worshipers. I suppose he must have been telling them about me, too, relaying what Ram had said, because they were soon turning and smiling and nodding at me, some of them making namastes, and I did the same back again, all the time feeling like a fraud. I wished they weren't so friendly. They were just making me feel bad about stealing their tiger.

But how was I going to steal it?

I scanned the room one last time, looking at the bowls of fruit, the stubby candles dripping wax, the bare-chested priests, the cross-legged pilgrims, and I looked at the hole, thinking of the tiger that must be down there, regretting that I hadn't had an opportunity to steal it yet, and an unexpected idea snuck into my mind.

One of the pilgrims must have thought I was smiling at him, because he grinned at me, then brought his hands together and did a namaste.

I did one back. I was getting pretty good at them by now. I could have stayed here all day doing namastes for everyone. But a plan had formed in my mind, and now it was time to make it happen. I turned to Suresh and said, "I'm worried about my uncle."

"Your uncle?"

"You know. The guy in the restaurant. Remember him?"

"Ah. Yes. I think he is your father."

"No, he's my uncle. Anyway, I'm worried about him. He's probably going to be worried about me, too."

"You want to go back?"

"Actually, I wonder if you could do me a favor. Will you go back? Will you go and find him and tell him where I am?"

Suresh was confused. "You want me to talk to your uncle?"

"Yes. Go back to the restaurant. Tell him I'm here. I'll come down soon. I just want to look around a bit more. I've never been to an Indian temple before. I'd like to spend another few minutes here. I'll be down soon."

"No problem. I will tell him."

"That's great. Thanks very much."

Suresh probably thought I was crazy—if I was so worried about my uncle, why didn't I go down to the restaurant and talk to him myself?—but he didn't ask any more questions, just left me alone and headed out of the temple. I gave him five minutes, checking the times on my phone, then walked after him, stealing a candle on my way out.

# 25

***I walked through the temple,*** holding the candle in one hand and shielding its flame with the other. A few spots of warm wax dripped into my palm. They didn't hurt.

Earlier, while I was following Suresh around the temple, I'd noticed a pile of timber stacked against a wall just outside the courtyard with the pool. Now I went back there.

I looked around, checking that no one was watching me.

The temple was a big place, filled with different buildings and courtyards. I didn't want to set fire to the whole place. I just wanted to make a little distraction, a plume of smoke and some scarlet flames, a small blaze to draw the guards away from the inner sanctum and give me a chance to sneak inside unseen.

This is probably a good moment to say, yes, I know I should have been feeling bad about what I was going to do. I should have been feeling guilty and ashamed. I don't exactly know why I wasn't. I guess it was simply because I was just too excited about grabbing the tiger. I didn't spend much time worrying about Suresh or Ram or any of the other people who loved this temple and spent their time here. Does that make me selfish? Yes. Am I embarrassed about it? I guess so. Did I worry about it? Not really. All my mind was taken up with what I was doing: preparing to commit arson without being caught.

I have some experience with arson. Once I set a shed on fire. That was a mistake, actually, but the experience taught me a few good tips about fires. All you need is a spark and some dry wood.

I placed the candle on the floor and arranged a few spindly twigs over the flame. They caught quickly. The wood must have been very dry. I coaxed it for a few moments till the fire was blazing merrily, then stood up and walked slowly and coolly away, as if I didn't have a care in the world.

I went into the next courtyard and sat down by the pool. Three old men were standing knee-deep in the water. Several more were squatting on the ground, sharing out a meal of rice and vegetable curry, served from little plastic bowls, eaten without cutlery. It smelled great.

My gran lives in an old folks' home packed with old folks who have nothing to do except watch TV or complain to the nurses.

Sitting by a pool and eating curry—this seemed like a much better way to be old.

I looked up at the trees but couldn't see the monkeys.

They must have gone hunting somewhere else in the temple. Unless they were hiding in the leaves, waiting for the perfect moment to pounce.

I heard shouting from another part of the temple.

*Here we go.*

The shouts grew louder and more intense. The old men at the pool clustered together, talking in screechy voices and gesticulating nervously. My nostrils tickled. That was from the smoke. The wood must have been burning well.

A man ran through the doorway and yelled some instructions. The old men gathered their belongings and headed for the exit. One of them turned and called out to me.

I waved at him. Like a dumb tourist.

That wasn't enough for the old man, who tottered across the cobbles and grabbed my sleeve.

"Come, come!" He sounded desperate.

I allowed myself to be pulled to my feet.

"You must be gone," he told me.

I didn't argue. I just followed him out of the courtyard. The corridors were full of people. The crowds bumped me apart from my savior, and I slipped unnoticed through a doorway and into the shadowy heart of the temple.

The elephant looked at me with baleful eyes. He was shifting from side to side, scuffing his huge feet on the flagstones. Could he smell the smoke? Or sense the panic? I wanted to reassure him. *Don't worry,* I would have said. *It's just a small fire on the other side of the temple. It won't come any-*

*where near here. You'll be fine.* Suddenly I felt a jolt of panic myself. What if I was wrong? What if the flames spread? What if they lashed through the temple, leaping from timber to timber, igniting bales of straw and dry walls, and burned the whole place to the ground? What if . . . ?

*Stop it. Stop worrying so much. It's only a small fire. This is a wooden building in a hot country, they must have fires all the time. They'll know exactly what to do. They'll put it out in a second. I'd better get the tiger before they do, or the whole thing will have been a waste of time.*

When I reached the inner sanctum, I found two priests arguing over a pile of documents. They stared at me, surprised. I must have looked just as surprised as them. There was no point trying to explain myself, so I simply doubled back and walked out again, then found a hiding place in the next room, sheltering behind a pillar.

I didn't have to wait very long. The men soon came out, their arms laden with papers they obviously wanted to save from the fire. I was watching them from behind the pillar, but neither of them even glanced in my direction.

This was my chance.

I ran into the inner sanctum.

It was empty. No priests. No pilgrims. No one but me. They'd probably be back in a moment to collect more scrolls or statues or whatever other valuables they had been protecting from the fire. What would they do if they caught me? Would they realize I'd started the fire? Would they arrest me? Or kill me? No time to worry about that now. *Just grab the tiger*, I told myself. *Worry about other things later.*

I shifted the candles and offerings to one side, then pulled the planks from the hole. I looked down. I couldn't see the bottom. I picked up a handful of fruit and dropped it into the hole. I counted. One. Two. Three. Four. *Splat!* How far was that? Far enough to hurt. I didn't want to plummet down there myself. I looked for handholds, footholds, anything at all to hold. Ah, yes. Look. A rock jutted out there. And another. I turned over onto my belly and slid my legs into the hole. My feet kicked, searching, and found a resting place. I lowered myself down. Peered into the shadow. Found another foothold. Then another.

I heard a voice above me.

Voices.

Getting louder. Coming closer.

I shimmied down the face of the rock. I don't know whether it was a well or just a hole in the ground, but it was deep enough to take my height and more. The darkness swallowed me up. My head was below the surface. I had disappeared.

I could distinguish two of the voices. Two men. They sounded hassled. They were moving fast. If they had glanced down the hole, they would have seen me immediately.

Did they notice the planks? Did they see that things had been moved?

If they did, they didn't care. They just grabbed whatever

they had come to collect, then jogged away. I heard their footsteps receding.

While I was waiting for them to leave, my eyes had adjusted to the darkness, and now I could see what was around me. I could see holes and bits of rock and a bundle of something, covered in dirt and dust.

Was that it?

I touched it gingerly.

My fingers brushed away what remained of some cloth. Over the years, the centuries, my ancestor's shirt had decayed into dust. It hardly existed anymore. But it had done its job, protecting the treasure. Here it was. A small tiger, the size of a grapefruit.

The metal felt cold. I don't know why I hadn't been expecting that.

The tiger was surprisingly heavy. I thought it was made of gold, but was gold really so heavy? What if it was actually made of solid stone? That wouldn't be worth much. Hey, that would be ironic: if I'd come all the way here and set fire to a temple just to steal a tiger that wasn't worth anything at all.

I could worry about that later. First I had to get out of here.

But how? I needed both hands to hold on. The tiger wouldn't fit in the pockets of my jeans, and I couldn't hold it with my teeth. So what was I going to do?

In the end, I put the tiger in the only place that it would go.

With two million dollars tucked in my pants, I scrambled up the wall and out of the hole. I rolled onto the ground and lay on my back for a moment, delighted to be alive. Then jumped to my feet and ran.

Out of the inner sanctum. Through the temple.

The elephant was straining against his chains but couldn't pull himself free.

*Sorry, pal. Gotta go.*

Once I got outside, I was shocked by how big the fire had grown. The flames must have rampaged over the dry wood. The air was thick with smoke. I couldn't feel the heat of the flames, but I could see their orange glare against the sky. The stones were warm under my feet, but that heat must have come from the sun, not the fire.

People were running back and forth. Some were shouting. A kid was standing alone, screaming. He must have been separated from his parents.

A chain of men and women were passing buckets back and forth along the corridor, full buckets going in one direction, empty ones returning in the other. The cobblestones were slippery from all the spilled water. I looked at their sweating faces and felt terrible about what I'd done. This wasn't what I'd intended. I wasn't planning to mess up their lives. I just wanted to get rid of those guards and buy myself some time. What should I do? Help them? Grab a bucket and make good my mistake? I wanted to. I really did. But I had a tiger in my pants and I had to get him out of here. Imagine what they'd do to me if they found out who I was—the guy who not only started this fire, but stole their treasure, too. They'd massacre me. I had to go.

As I came closer to the gates, the crowd thickened, bodies squeezing together to fit through the narrow doorway.

I was carried along by the flood of people rushing down the stairs, trying to escape from the smoke and flames. Ahead of us, I could see a single person pushing the other way, heading up the hill rather than down. We were almost face-to-face before I realized who he was. He must have recognized me at the same moment, because he stopped in the middle of the steps, apparently unaware of the bodies buffeting past.

"You are fine?" asked Ram.

"Yes, yes, I'm fine."

"Good." His eyes flickered over me. I searched for any sign of suspicion, but all I could see was concern. "You must go. Get away from here. The fire is dangerous. You understand?"

"Yes." I stared at him, words formed on my lips, an apology, an explanation, but I couldn't say any of it. I just stood there helplessly, the stench of smoke in my nostrils.

"I must go," he said. "I have to help. Goodbye, Mister Tom."

"Bye," I muttered back, and then he was gone, striding up the hill toward the temple.

Had he suspected anything?

Did he know what I'd done?

I took one final look at the temple. I glimpsed what might

have been the back of Ram's head, and then he was gone, swallowed up among the mass of bodies pouring down the hill. The flames were rising ever higher, carrying a cascade of sparks into the sky, and I thought about Ram, and I felt terrible. I could have gone after him and helped deal with the fire.

No, not *the* fire. *My* fire. The one I'd started. The one that was going to tear down his temple, his work, his home.

Shouldn't I help put it out?

Shouldn't I join the chain of men and women passing buckets from the pool to the heart of the flames?

I would have if I hadn't had a tiger down my pants. I'd shoot down the hill, I told myself, and give the tiger to my uncle, or find a decent hiding place for it, then come back up again and help clean up the mess I'd made.

# 26

**I sprinted down the hill,** taking the stairs two at a time, my bare feet slapping against the crooked stone steps.

I arrived at the bottom to find a crowd of a hundred people, maybe many more, gazing upward, watching the flames on the top of the hill. Suddenly I heard my uncle shouting, "Tom! Tom! Over here! Tom!"

He pushed through the crowd to meet me. Tanya followed just behind. They both overflowed with questions, wanting to know where I'd been and what I'd seen.

I couldn't tell the truth with Tanya there. "It just happened so quickly," I said, trying to sound shocked. "Suddenly the whole place was full of smoke." I shook my head as if the experience had been too much for me.

Tanya was completely taken in. She gave me a hug and promised everything was going to be fine. My uncle didn't seem suspicious either. He patted me on the shoulder. "Come on, kid. Let's get out of here. Apparently there's a good hotel in Srirangapatna. We'll go and check in now. You'll feel a lot better once you've had a shower."

I tried to get a moment alone with Uncle Harvey, but it was impossible. Tanya wouldn't let go of him. He wouldn't let go of her, either. The two of them walked arm in arm down the street, Uncle Harvey trying to persuade Tanya that he should be allowed to carry her rucksack, and her giggling, saying she was stronger than he was, she could carry her own bag and his too.

"We'll arm-wrestle for it," said Uncle Harvey.

"Here? Now? I'm ready."

"We need a table. Let's have a competition when we get to the hotel. Loser pays for dinner."

"I will beat you both," said Tanya. "You have to remember, Harvey, I'm an Israeli. I do my national service. I know how to fight."

"So do I," said Uncle Harvey.

That would have been my moment to say, *Wait a minute, let's go back up the hill, I want to help the priests put out the fire,* and I wish I'd said exactly that, but I didn't. I still had the tiger in my pants. I wanted to get him out, and even more important, I wanted to tell my uncle that I had it. I couldn't say anything in front of Tanya. I glanced back at the temple and thought about Ram, and felt bad, then ran after my uncle.

Suresh had been waiting with his rickshaw. He was staring anxiously at the sky, watching the plume of smoke rising from the temple. As soon as he saw us, he hurried forward, unable to keep back his questions. "What is happening? How big is the fire?"

I told him as little as I'd told the others.

"What of the temple?" he asked.

"What about it?"

"It is hurt? It is OK?"

I could hear the panic in his voice and saw tears streaked through the dust on his face.

I wished I could convince him not to care so much about the imaginary god in its hole. *It can't possibly help your mom,* I wanted to say, *because it doesn't even exist. Forget it. I've got some good news for you. There's a tiger in my pants that is worth a couple of million dollars, and once we've sold it, I'm going to come back here and give you some money and you'll be able to pay for your mom's chemo yourself.* But I kept those thoughts to myself and simply said that the fire had only been in one small part of the temple, far away from the inner sanctum.

"You are sure?" he asked, suddenly hopeful.

"I'm sure. Your god's safe."

He wiped away his tears and tried to smile.

There was just enough room for all three of us in the back of the rickshaw, Tanya in the middle with a Trelawney on either side, her rucksack and my uncle's bag at our feet.

My uncle called out, "Home, James, and don't spare the horses."

"Excuse me, sir?" Suresh was puzzled.

"Don't take any notice of him," I said. "He's just being an idiot."

"No problem. But where to go?"

"That hotel in Srirangapatna," said my uncle. "The one you recommended."

"Ah, yes, sir. Right away."

Suresh turned the key in the ignition. The engine coughed to life. Some startled birds flew out of a nearby tree. And we were off, bouncing down the road and chugging all the way to Srirangapatna.

*Forget the hotel,* I wanted to say. *We've got much more important things to do. We've got to go to Bangalore and sell this tiger for two million dollars.* But I kept quiet. I didn't want Tanya to know what we were doing. I didn't know her, and certainly didn't trust her. I didn't think she was a spy of Marko's—although the thought had crossed my mind—but I didn't want her knowing our business anyway. Much more important, I never wanted Suresh to discover what I'd done.

I leaned out of the rickshaw and looked behind us. No one was following us. On the top of the hill, a faint orange glow silhouetted the walls of the temple.

Sitting back down, I got a glimpse of Suresh's face. He looked haunted, even frightened. *Don't worry about the temple,* I thought. *That temple never would have helped your mom. She needs chemo and a decent doctor. If all goes well, I'll be back here tomorrow to get her exactly that.*

Sixty bone-juddering minutes later, we chugged into the center of Srirangapatna and stopped outside the Hotel Krishna. Even there, I couldn't talk to my uncle. He rushed inside and negotiated a price for two rooms, then arranged to meet Tanya in an hour to wander around town.

A porter had come out of the hotel to carry our baggage, but Uncle Harvey waved him away. "We can carry our own bags." Disappointed, the porter slouched back inside.

Suresh was waiting patiently to be paid. He was a different person to the one who had picked us up earlier in the day. Then he'd been cheerful, optimistic, ready for anything. Now he was about to cry again.

I don't know if my uncle took pity on him or was really impressed by his skills as a chauffeur, but he pulled out a bundle of notes from his wallet. "Here you go," he said. "Thanks for everything."

Suresh's face lit up. He grabbed my uncle's hand. "Thank you, Mister Harvey. You are a very good man."

"Don't mention it," said Uncle Harvey.

Suresh grabbed my hand and thanked me, too, which raised my guilt levels.

He stuffed the cash into one of his pockets, then pulled something from another. "Please, you will take my card. If you need one more driver, you will call me."

I took Suresh's card, which was actually just a scrap of paper scribbled with his name and number. I stuffed it in my pocket, promising to call him if we ever came back to Srirangapatna. I didn't tell him why I'd really be calling him; I didn't want him to get too excited. But I was sure I'd be on the phone in a day or two, talking to Suresh, telling him that I wanted to know where to send enough money to make his mom well again.

He jumped in his rickshaw and drove away. I suppose he couldn't wait to present Uncle Harvey's cash to his mom. How much medicine would it buy? Enough to help her? Or just enough to stop the pain for a few days?

I remembered my mom's friend Sandra, the one who died of cancer. I only met her a couple of times, but one of her kids was good friends with Grace, so we got constant updates. Mom talked about her a lot, always in the same hushed tone.

Her daughters set up a website in her memory. They organized a five-mile fun run and sent an email around, asking people to sponsor them. I gave Grace fifty cents a mile. On the site, there was a photo taken while Sandra was lying on her hospital bed. She looked like someone had stuck a tube down her throat and sucked the life out of her.

I followed my uncle into the hotel and up to our room, which was small and cold and smelled as if the last person staying here hadn't flushed the toilet.

Uncle Harvey dumped his bag on the bed. "You need a shower," he said. "Your face is covered in soot. Your clothes, too. We're going to have to buy you some more."

"And shoes."

He looked at my bare feet. "Where are your shoes?"

"In the temple. You have to take them off when you go inside."

"I'll buy you some nice new sandals. You can borrow a shirt of mine. You'll have to wear those same jeans and go barefoot for now. My shoes won't fit you. Have a shower, put this on, and we'll go out with Tanya to buy you a new wardrobe." He offered me the shirt that he'd pulled from his bag. "You're lucky she's here. She'll pick some nice stuff. Here, take this." That was when he noticed what I was holding in the palm of my hand. "What's that?"

"What does it look like?"

"I don't know. What is it?"

"Guess."

"A stone."

"Guess again."

"I don't like these games. Just tell me what it is."

"Can't you guess?"

"I just said no."

"Try."

"Fine. Here. Let me have a look." He took it out of my hand. "It is, um . . . Oh, I don't know. A stone covered in gunk." He scraped off some of the dirt with his fingernail. "That's funny, it looks like . . ." His voice faded away. He glanced at me. Then back at the shimmering jewel that his cleaning had just exposed. Now his voice was more serious. "What is this?"

"You still can't guess?"

"Don't mess about. What is this?"

"It's a tiger, Uncle Harvey."

"Where did you get it?"

"From a hole on the top of a hill."

"This hole—was it in that temple?"

"Yes."

"Did anyone see you?"

"No. That's why I had to start the fire. To get everyone out of there."

"You started that fire?"

"Yes."

"You set fire to the temple?"

"Yes."

"I don't believe it," said Uncle Harvey.

"I didn't mean to," I explained. "I just started a small fire to distract the guards. I didn't think it would turn into that towering inferno. I just wanted to make a blaze that was big enough to make them panic. It worked, too. The guards came running. So did the priests. They left the inner sanctum unguarded. So I shot in there and grabbed the tiger and got out of there before anyone noticed anything."

My uncle looked at me, his mouth twisted into a strange little smile. I couldn't tell what it meant. What he said next was strange, too. "I hope you're ready for who you're going to be."

"What does that mean?"

"It means exactly what I said."

I repeated his words to myself. *"I hope you're ready for who you're going to be."* Then I shook my head. "No, I don't know what that means."

"You'll work it out soon enough." He was grinning more

straightforwardly now, his face breaking open with the happy smile of a man who can already see a million dollars in his bank account.

Then he rushed into the bathroom and washed two hundred years of dirt down the drain.

# 27

**The guy who owned** the hotel tried to make Uncle Harvey pay for the night, even though we'd only been in the room for a few minutes. Tanya came into the lobby when they were arguing and asked what was going on. Uncle Harvey started looking a bit hassled. "We have to go," he said.

"Where?"

"Back to Bangalore. Just for the night."

"Oh."

"Give me a moment and I'll explain everything." Then he glanced at me, meeting my eyes for a moment as if to say: *Don't worry, I won't tell her the truth, I'll make something up.*

He managed to get us out of the hotel without having to pay. As for Tanya—I don't know what he said to her, but whatever it was, she wasn't impressed. Uncle Harvey kissed her on both cheeks. He tried to kiss her on the lips, too, but she dodged out of the way.

"I'll call you once we've finished our business in Bangalore," he said. "We can meet up there. Stay in a nice hotel. Go out for dinner."

"Maybe," said Tanya. "Bye, Tom. Have fun."

"Thanks," I said. "And you."

A rickshaw took us to the train station. I would have liked to get a ride with Suresh, but he'd gone.

The clerk in the ticket office told us that the Mysore–Bengaluru express would be passing through in forty minutes. We bought two tickets, then ducked outside and found a street lined with clothes shops. I said I only needed fresh underwear, a T-shirt, and some sneakers, but Uncle Harvey insisted on buying me a whole new wardrobe.

"We're meeting a billionaire," he said. "We don't want to look like tramps."

"I don't get it. Why would J.J. care what I look like? We've got the tiger. He wants it. Isn't that enough?"

"Not at all." Uncle Harvey held up a shirt against me, then winced and put it back on the shelf. "If you look like you need to sell, your price goes down. When we meet J.J., we have to look like we don't need the money. We'd like him to buy it, but if he doesn't, we don't care. That's the only way we're going to get a decent price. Appearance is everything. That's the first rule of business. Ah, this one looks perfect. Here. Try it on."

We hurried back to the station carrying our purchases and boarded our train. It was packed, but we managed to find ourselves a couple of seats by the window. Once the train left the station, I took my shopping bags to the bathroom. It wasn't the perfect place to change your clothes— there was a big pool of what I hoped was water in the middle of the floor—but I managed to do it without getting my new pair of pants wet. When I returned to the carriage, my uncle looked me up and down, then told me to tuck my shirt in. Finally he nodded. "You'll do."

"You mean, I look cool?"

"No. But you'll do."

"Gee, thanks."

He went to the bathroom and got changed too, and, I had to admit, he looked dapper. Gone were the dusty pants and the grubby shirt, replaced by black trousers, black shoes, a white shirt, and a dark brown jacket. These were the clothes that he'd worn to Grandpa's funeral, but he didn't look deathly. If you saw him striding briskly along the street, you would have thought he was a successful businessman on his way to do a deal. He sat down opposite me and pulled out his phone. He said he had to do some research. I asked what that meant. He wouldn't tell me, but in a few minutes he said, "Come and look at this."

"What is it?"

"Come here and I'll show you."

He'd connected to YouTube. When he pressed Play, the screen lit up with a bright orange logo, a capital J imposed over a roaring tiger.

"*The Jaragami Corporation is one of India's most remarkable success stories,*" said a deep voice. "*But this extraordinary company was originally nothing more than an idea, a vision in the imagination of one mathematical prodigy and business visionary, the company's founder and owner, Jalata Jaragami.*"

The screen now showed a slim man standing at a podium, addressing a conference.

The voiceover continued: "*Jaragami started his company with only a few thousand rupees, borrowed from a family member, and traded from his own bedroom in a modest suburb of Bengaluru. Today, the Jaragami Corporation employs more than one hundred thousand people in India and abroad, and has an annual turnover of more than five billion U.S. dollars.*"

More footage followed of Jalata Jaragami shaking hands with various famous people. I recognized only two of them, Bill Gates and Barack Obama, but Uncle Harvey told me the names of the others.

The screen showed a picture of a young Indian boy with glasses. The narrator said, "*Jalata Jaragami learned to program a computer at the age of six. He started his first software company when he was eleven and earned his first million rupees only three days after his fourteenth birthday.*"

"You'd better hurry," said Uncle Harvey.

"I'm going to earn my first million today."

"So you are."

The carriage was full of people. Some of them were reading books or newspapers and others were staring at their own phones, but a couple of them now crowded around my uncle, staring at the film, and soon others joined them too. I could hear them whispering in their own language. One of them said, "Jaragami, yes?" When I agreed, he gave me a big smile. "Very rich man."

The film was still playing. After a few minutes of boring information about J.J.'s company, its computers and their software, the narrator offered one little snippet of personal information about the founder, owner, and boss of the company.

"*Jalata Jaragami is not just a wealthy businessman and a generous philanthropist,*" said the deep-voiced narrator. "*He is also a collector of valuable art and antiques, with a particular interest in India's ancient heritage. Over the past decade, he has amassed the world's finest collection of material related to Tipu Sultan, one of the foremost fighters in the battle against British rule of the subcontinent. After the battle of Seringapatam and the murder of Tipu Sultan by British forces, his treasures were stolen and scattered around the world. Jalata Jaragami is bringing these treasures back here to India, where they belong, creating a magnificent museum devoted to one of the foremost figures in the history of the subcontinent.*"

Accompanying the last words, the screen had shown a series of images: a painting of a man in a turban; a sword with intricate carvings along the handle; a large white building surrounded by trees; a vast, airy room inside the museum, with pictures and objects hanging around the wall.

Uncle Harvey paused the video.

We stared at the image of J.J.'s museum.

In the center of the room, squatting like an immense frog, was a large, ornate throne, its seat covered with scarlet cushions, its back lined with eight spears. Seven of them were topped with little tiger statues. The eighth remained empty.

# 28

**Night had fallen** by the time we arrived in Bangalore, and in the darkness the streets seemed even fuller, packed with a billion cars, buses, and trucks, and a billion people, too, dodging between the lanes of traffic.

A taxi drove us from the station to the business district and dropped us at the foot of an enormous tower. I tipped back my head and stared at the thousands of windows above us, every one of them blazing bright light. It was the type of skyscraper that you might find in New York, filled with busy office workers making money, money, money.

Over the entrance stood a line of huge proud steel letters.

JARAGAMI

Uncle Harvey and I strolled into the entrance lobby. The huge glass doors slid silently shut behind us. I wondered if Marko had been here. Was this where he came to get his orders? Did he come here to meet J.J.? Or was there no real connection between them? Did J.J. just order one of his servants to get the tigers using any means necessary, not wanting to know what would actually happen? Would Marko be here now? I wasn't sure if I dreaded the idea of seeing him or relished it. I wanted to confront him, yes, and take my revenge, but he scared me too—I don't mind admitting that. And if we ran into him here, it wouldn't even be a fair fight; he'd have all the advantages. This was his territory. We wouldn't have a hope.

Several security guards lingered by the entrance, watching our progress. Long wooden batons hung from their belts. That explained the lack of beggars.

The temperature outside was tropical, even after dark, but the lobby was so efficiently air-conditioned, we could have been back in Ireland.

Six gorgeous women were sitting behind a long, shiny desk. Any of them could have gotten a job as a model. Three were answering calls on their headsets, two more were talking to visitors, and the last in line smiled at us. "Good evening, gentlemen. Can I help you?"

"I very much hope so," said my uncle, giving her a flirtatious smile. We'd only been apart from Tanya for a couple of hours, but he'd forgotten her already.

The receptionist remained strictly professional. "Who are you here to see?"

"Jalata Jaragami."

"Very good, sir. Do you have an appointment?"

"No."

"Then I am afraid Mr. Jaragami will be unable to see you. Would you like to discuss your business with someone else?"

"No, thanks. I just want to see Mr. Jaragami."

Finally the receptionist smiled. Now she understood who we were: a pair of dumb tourists who had wandered into the wrong place by mistake. "If you would like to make your way to the Welcome Chamber, you can see an audiovisual presentation about Mr. Jaragami and the Jaragami Corporation. Please, I will have someone show you the way." She beckoned to one of the guards.

"I don't want to see an audiovisual presentation," replied Uncle Harvey. "I'd like to see Mr. Jaragami."

"I'm sorry, sir, but that will not be possible. Mr. Jaragami is a very busy man."

"I'm sure he is. But I promise you, when he knows what I've got, he will want to see me."

"I could connect you to one of his secretaries if you would like to make an appointment."

"Yes, please."

The receptionist pressed a button and spoke into her headpiece. Then she picked up a phone and handed it to my uncle. "Please, you will tell this man why you wish to see Mr. Jaragami."

Uncle Harvey took the phone and explained about the tiger. Then he did it again. And again. And once more. Each time, he was talking to someone more senior, higher up the tower, closer to J.J. himself. Finally he handed the receiver back to the receptionist. "He wants to talk to you."

When she next looked at us, there was a different expression in her eyes. I thought I could detect a mixture of surprise and respect. We weren't the dumb tourists she'd taken us for.

"Mr. Bharati will see you at once," she said. "He is the personal assistant to Mr. Jaragami. Please, follow this man."

A man in a uniform led us to the elevators. We stepped inside. The buttons went up to 30. Our escort pressed 29. The doors closed and we were swept smoothly and soundlessly toward the top of the tower.

When we arrived on the twenty-ninth floor, another guide was waiting, wearing an even smarter uniform. This one took us through a maze of corridors to a meeting room with a long table, eight chairs, and a big window with a view of the city. On a sideboard there were glasses and cups and drinks and a plate piled high with strange-looking snacks, not quite samosas and not quite croissants, but something in between. The guide told us to wait.

We stood around for five minutes, then the door opened and a heavyset man marched into the room. He had big hands, a steady smile, and very dark skin.

"Good evening," he said. "Welcome to the Jaragami Corporation. My name is Vivek Bharati. You are Tom and Harvey Trelawney, that is correct? If you don't mind me asking, which of you is which?"

We introduced ourselves. He asked us to sit down, although he managed to make it sound more like an order than a request, then told us that he was Jalata Jaragami's advisor. "I am his right-hand man. When you are speaking to me, you are speaking to Mr. Jaragami. I am most interested to hear that you have the eighth tiger from Tipu Sultan's throne. We have been searching everywhere for this, not just in India, but all over the world. May I see it, please?"

"I'm afraid not," said Uncle Harvey.

"No?"

"No."

"But, why not?"

"I'm only going to show it to Jalata Jaragami himself."

"You have nothing to fear, Mr. Trelawney. As I have told you already, when you are speaking to me, you are speaking to Mr. Jaragami. What you are showing to me, you are showing to him. I am his eyes and ears. Please, let me see the tiger."

Uncle Harvey shook his head. "If your boss really wants it, he's going to have to talk to me himself."

"I am confused, Mr. Trelawney. Don't you want to sell this tiger?"

"That's why I'm here."

"Then you must to show it to me."

"I've told you already, that's not going to happen. I'll only show it to Jaragami."

"He will not see you."

"Then I won't waste any more of your time." My uncle nodded to me. "Come on, Tom. Let's go back to the hotel."

I almost said, *Hotel? What hotel?* Luckily my brain moved a little quicker than that. I grabbed my bag and stood up.

"Wait a minute," said Bharati. "There is no need for any hasty actions. I will talk to Mr. Jaragami and ask if he wishes to speak to you."

# 29

***I thought we'd only*** be waiting there for a couple of minutes, but we were actually alone for about an hour. I spent the time pacing up and down, thinking about what my uncle had said to me. *I hope you're ready for who you're going to be.* What did that mean? Who was I going to be? Would I be like him, forgetting about my grandfather's killer, only caring about money? Was that how real Trelawneys behaved? If so, did I really want to be like that? No, of course not. I didn't care about the money. Sure, no one was threatening to break my legs, but that wasn't the point. I wouldn't care even if they were. I just wanted to find Grandpa's killer.

My uncle sat patiently at the table, reading stuff on his phone. When I asked what he was doing, he replied, "Research."

"What kind of research?"

"I'm learning about J.J. Always be prepared. That's the first rule of business."

"I thought the first rule of business was—"

"Oh, stop it. Don't ask me to be logical, that's not my style. Do you want to know the real first rule of business?"

"Yes."

"Earn more money than you spend. It is a rule that I have broken almost every day of my life. But not today." He laughed suddenly.

"What's so funny?"

"Nothing."

"What is it?"

"Just a message from a girl."

"I thought you were doing research."

"I am. But I'm sending a few messages, too."

He tapped the screen.

Research—yeah, right. He was just flirting with some girl on the other side of the world.

I went back to staring out of the window. I didn't bother telling him what I was thinking about. I didn't want to talk to him about Marko. I knew what he'd say. *Shut up, don't worry, it's all going to be fine.* I didn't want to have another argument about the rights and wrongs of chasing the money rather than Grandpa's murderer.

Around the time that I was beginning to wonder if we'd been forgotten, the door swung open and seven people marched into the room, four men and three women. I was relieved to see that Marko wasn't among them.

If I hadn't recognized Jalata Jaragami from the YouTube video, I never would have guessed he was the richest of the seven, the boss of them all. The others looked far more slick and important than him, the men broad-shouldered and handsome, the women elegant and beautiful, their necks and fingers dotted with discreet jewelry. J.J. himself was a nerdy little man with scruffy sneakers, faded jeans, a white T-shirt, and small, round glasses. He must have noticed my uncle and me, but he paid no attention to us, carrying on his conversation with Bharati as if we weren't even there.

One of the women was talking into her phone. Another was jotting notes on a tablet. The third shook my uncle's hand, then mine.

"Mr. Jaragami is very pleased to meet you," she said.

"He hasn't actually met us yet," I said.

She ignored me. "You will appreciate that Mr. Jaragami is a busy man, so he will be grateful if you can state your business quickly and concisely. Do you understand?"

"Perfectly," said Uncle Harvey.

"Thank you. Mr. Jaragami has been briefed already. He knows you have possession of an object which interests him."

"You mean the tiger?" I said.

Again she ignored me. "As you know, Mr. Jaragami is very keen to see this object. However, he will also need to see some authentication of the object's provenance. Are you able to provide any evidence of— "

She broke off in midsentence as Jaragami swooped down on us. "Hello, hello, thank you for waiting, I hope you haven't been here long." He offered his hand to my uncle. "Mr. Trelawney, how very good to meet you."

"You too, Mr. Jaragami," said my uncle.

"Please call me J.J. Everyone else does, especially non-Indians. The pronunciation of my true name appears to perplex them." Jaragami turned to me and pressed my hand between his palms. "And you must be Tom. How are you enjoying India?" He managed to make it sound as if he owned the whole place.

"I haven't seen much of it," I said. "We only arrived yesterday."

"You came from England?"

"We were in Ireland."

"Near enough. How is the weather?"

"It's cold."

"And raining?"

"Yes."

"Of course it is." J.J. grinned. "I love everything about England except the weather. Even the food isn't as bad as people say, but the weather is truly abhorrent. I spent a whole year there, studying at Oxford, and it rained almost every single day."

"What an amazing coincidence," said Uncle Harvey. "I was at Oxford too."

"You were at Oxford University?"

"That's right. The happiest years of my life. Which college were you at?"

"I thought you went to Edinburgh University," said J.J. "Although you were only there for a year, is that not right? Then you were forced to leave after failing your exams."

Uncle Harvey was very rarely at a loss for words, but this was one of those occasions. He finally managed to stammer, "H-how do you know that?"

"Information is my business, Mr. Trelawney. Give me a computer terminal and I will tell you what is happening anywhere and everywhere on the planet. Knowledge is power. You know this phrase? If it had not been said already, I would have to say it for myself, because it is so remarkably truthful. While you have been waiting here, I have learned everything about you, Mr. Harvey Humperdinck Trelawney."

"Your middle name is Humperdinck?" I said. "Why did no one ever tell me that?"

My uncle didn't react. I guess he was still in shock.

"I know where you have lived," continued J.J. "I know where you have traveled. I even know the state of your finances. Which are not looking too good, if you don't mind me saying so."

"That's why I'm here," said my uncle. He'd managed to pull himself together and was smiling again, although he still looked rattled.

"You know about my interest in Tipu Sultan," continued J.J. "You know I have acquired seven of the eight tigers from his throne. You come here and you say you are the owner, the possessor, of the last of them, the eighth tiger, the object that I covet more than anything else in the world. You say all this, Mr. Trelawney, yet you refuse to show this tiger to my closest advisor. You can imagine why I am intrigued,

Mr. Trelawney, but also a little suspicious. Now I am here. And I should like to see this tiger."

Uncle Harvey paused for a moment before replying. He seemed to be thinking. Perhaps he was simply enjoying the moment, taking his chance to tantalize a billionaire. Did he have a strategy? Did he really know what he was doing? I hoped so. He kneeled down, unzipped his bag, and pulled out the tiger. It was wrapped in one of his white shirts. He dropped the shirt back in the bag. "Here you are. The eighth of Tipu Sultan's tigers, taken from his throne on the night of May the fourth, 1799."

"May I?" asked J.J.

"Please." Uncle Harvey handed the tiger to him.

J.J. took it carefully, lovingly, as if it were a delicate flower and not a lump of metal, then turned it over and over and over again, inspecting it from every angle.

His assistants had put away their phones and now all their attention was focused on their boss, waiting for his reaction.

Finally he lifted his head from the tiger and looked at my uncle. To my relief, I saw he was smiling. "This is very nice," he said.

"It's a beautiful piece," replied Uncle Harvey.

"It certainly is. It looks perfect. But there is such a thing as too perfect. If something is too perfect, I can't help feeling suspicious."

"It might just be perfect."

"Mr. Trelawney, every day, people are coming to me, promising that they have what I want. They say they have found a sword which belonged to Tipu Sultan. If not a sword, then a dagger, a cloak, a jewel. I send none of them away. Instead I ask an expert to examine what they have brought me. He will check its provenance. Ninety-nine times out of a hundred, they are forgeries. Is your tiger going to be any different?"

"This is the real thing," said Uncle Harvey.

"Then why don't I own it?"

"Do you own all of Tipu Sultan's treasures?"

"Not all, but most."

"But you don't have his eighth tiger?"

J.J. smiled. "Touché. So tell me about your tiger. Where is it from? How do you come to own it?"

"Don't you know already?" I asked.

J.J. was staring at me, surprised, as if it hadn't occurred to him that I could talk. "How would I know?"

"Didn't Marko tell you?" I said.

"Marko? Who is Marko?"

"Marko Malinkovic. Doesn't he work for you?"

"I have never heard of him."

That was when Uncle Harvey stepped in. "Please excuse my nephew. He's had a long flight and he's feeling confused. Let me tell you about this tiger. You wanted to hear about its history. It was taken by a British soldier, who stole it and hid it, and it's stayed hidden ever since. His name was Horatio Trelawney and was my great-great-great-great-great-grandfather. He was among the first group of soldiers who looted Tipu's palace. He and his comrades broke up the throne and stole the tigers, taking one each. The tiger was passed to his son, and his son's son, down through the generations, until it reached me."

"All this time," said J.J., "for all these years, none of them thought of selling it?"

"They respected my great-great-great-great-great-grandfather's wishes," replied Uncle Harvey. "Horatio insisted the tiger had to stay in the family."

"So why are you selling it now?" asked J.J.

"Because I need the money," said Uncle Harvey.

J.J. laughed. "You know, this does sound interesting."

At that moment, one of his advisors gave him a discreet nod. He didn't acknowledge her in any way, but he must have understood the signal, because he said to us, "Do you mind if we walk while we talk?"

Without waiting for an answer, he strode briskly toward the door, expecting us to follow. Uncle Harvey grabbed my elbow. He gave me a look. He didn't need to say anything. I understood exactly what he meant. Shut up about Marko. Remember what we agreed. Then he was hurrying after J.J. I went with him. J.J. carried on talking as soon as we caught up with him.

"I have a meeting now," he said. "But I'd like to take your tiger to my museum. There, I have experts. They will authenticate this piece. If it is the real thing, we can discuss a deal."

"I'm afraid that's not possible," said my uncle.

"You don't want to sell it?"

"I want to sell it. But I won't let it out of my sight."

"Come to the museum too. You can meet the curator and have a look around."

"I'd like that. May I?" Uncle Harvey held out his hand for the tiger, but J.J. pretended not to notice.

Two elevators were waiting, the doors already open, a man standing inside each of them, ready to the press the buttons for us. J.J. led us into one and the rest of his entourage crammed into the other. The man in our elevator pressed the button marked 30. We went up a single floor in less than a second. Then the doors opened again and we stepped out onto a wide, flat roof. The sky was dark, but the air was still warm and a hot breeze whisked over us. The city was spread out around us, a million lights twinkling in hundreds of tall tower blocks.

In the middle of the roof, a slim black helicopter was waiting, its rotors whipping the warm air. Through the windshield, I could see two pilots hunched over the controls.

J.J.'s entourage spilled out of the other elevator. One of the women peeled away from the group and came to meet us.

"Meera will drive you to the museum," said J.J. "My experts are waiting there to authenticate this tiger. They will make sure that it is the real thing. I shall meet you there as soon as I can."

I couldn't believe it. Weren't we going in the helicopter?

We weren't.

Without even bothering to say goodbye, J.J. was already hurrying across the roof.

Uncle Harvey charged after him. "The tiger!"

Reluctantly J.J. turned around and handed the tiger to my uncle. He took it with both hands, then yelled to be heard over the noise of the rotors. "We have to talk about one more thing."

"Oh, yes? What's that?"

"Money."

"Money?" J.J. spread his arms wide, encompassing the tower, the helicopter, the city, perhaps the entire country, as if he owned it all. "If your tiger is *the* tiger, I will give you as much money as you want."

"How much is that?" asked Uncle Harvey.

"Wait till we authenticate the tiger, then we can talk about money."

With that he was gone again, this time not giving my uncle the chance to call him back.

We stood on the edge of the roof, watching J.J. settle himself into his seat, strap a belt over his shoulders, and clamp a pair of big headphones onto his ears.

I waited for him to turn and wave, or even cast a glance in our direction, but he appeared to have forgotten us already and was peering at a computer on his knees. The glowing screen lit up the lenses of his glasses, giving the illusion, just for a moment, that his eyes were on fire.

# 30

**Once the helicopter had** sped away, its lights dwindling into the darkness, Meera escorted us into the elevator and down to the main lobby. Uncle Harvey gave her all his best pickup lines, but she seemed much more interested in her phone than him.

When the elevator reached the ground floor, Meera marched us across the lobby, her high heels clattering on the polished floor. We followed a few paces behind.

My uncle winked at me.

A long black limousine was parked next to the tower, a driver in a sober uniform standing by the open door. I stared through the blacked-out windows and wondered who might be inside. Only when Meera nodded to the driver did I understand it was for us.

We settled on the long back seat.

Meera opened a fridge built into the door. "What would you like?"

I had a Coke. Uncle Harvey took a beer.

It was quite a contrast to Suresh's rickshaw.

*I could get used to this,* I thought. Then I remembered Marko. Had he and J.J. sprawled against these seats? Had they driven through the city, drinking beer, discussing how to get the letters from my grandfather? What had Marko asked for? What had J.J. ordered him to do? What did they decide?

We drove through the city for about an hour, moving slowly through traffic jams, kids clustered around the windows, knocking on the glass, trying to get our attention. One of them looked so like Suresh that I thought he'd actually followed us here. What would he be doing now? Eating supper with his mom and his brother and sisters? Or driving around the streets, searching for a fare, trying to earn a few more rupees for his mom's medicines?

Meera spent the whole journey on the phone, carrying on conversations in at least two languages and maybe several more, never giving Uncle Harvey a chance to talk to her.

When she was deep in a particularly intense discussion, Uncle Harvey turned to me and, speaking almost in a whisper, asked what I had been playing at.

"I wanted to know about Marko," I replied.

"We made a deal, remember. One thing at a time. First we'll sell the tiger, then we'll worry about Marko."

"Don't you want to know the truth?"

"I want to see him punished for what he did. Of course I do. But we can't get to him, whereas we can do something about the tiger. And once we've got the money, we'll be in a much better position to deal with the police." He glanced at

Meera. She was still deep in conversation and didn't seem at all interested in us. There was no way she could have heard what we were saying, but he carried on talking in a whisper that seemed even quieter than before. "Don't worry, Tom. I'm not going to forget about Marko, but I want to sell this tiger first."

I wasn't convinced. "We shouldn't have come here. We should have gone straight to the airport and taken it home. Then we could have kept it *and* told the police about Marko. If J.J. is so hot to buy it, he'll come and meet us there. That would be perfect. If he had something to do with Grandpa's murder, the police could arrest him too."

"They'll never arrest him without evidence. Anyway, I can't imagine he had anything to do with the murder. Billionaires usually have subtler ways of getting what they want. If Marko did murder my father, I can't imagine he was following orders."

"If? What do you mean, if?"

"You don't know what Marko actually did. He might just have been showing off, trying to scare you."

"He was telling the truth," I said. I was sure about that. I remembered Marko's eyes. Yes, he'd wanted to scare me, but he hadn't been lying. "Let's get out, Uncle Harvey. Let's go to the airport. We can take the tiger with us. It's the perfect solution."

"You've forgotten one thing," said Uncle Harvey. "I need to go home with at least ninety grand, or an angry Glaswegian is going to break both my legs. I promise you, Tom, once we've got the cash, I'll do everything I can to track down Marko and make him pay for what he's done."

I wanted to argue with him, but I knew it wouldn't make any difference. He'd already made up his mind. What should I do? What could I do? Call the police? They'd just take me home and give me back to Mom and Dad. Then I wouldn't have a chance of getting revenge for Grandpa's death.

I slumped back in my seat and stared angrily out the window. If only I could have come here alone. That's the problem with traveling with someone else. You have to do what they want, rather than what you want. Yes, yes, I know, I wouldn't have gotten as far as the airport without Uncle Harvey, let alone to the temple, but I couldn't help wishing he'd leave me alone now.

Then I had an idea.

I tried not to smile. I didn't want to give Uncle Harvey any hint of what I was thinking.

The more I thought about my idea, the more I knew I had to do it. I just had to. It was as simple as that. Yes, I know, I'd made a deal with him, but some deals have to be broken.

He'd be furious. I might even be the cause of him getting his legs broken. But I thought not. Uncle Harvey was a smart guy. He got himself in bad situations, but he always managed to get out of them. He'd find some way to pay off his angry Glaswegian.

One day, he might even thank me.

We emerged out of the crowded streets and accelerated down a highway. We came to fields, then a thick woodland. A high wall ran along one side of the road. The driver slowed down. Six or seven chickens were blocking the road. He hooted and they squawked out of our way. We were alongside a village of rickety shacks built from loose bricks and bundles of hay. A moment later, we came to a tall steel gate, which opened to let out a uniformed guard. He tipped his cap at our driver.

I asked Meera why that village was here, so close to the museum.

"They are the families who used to live on this site," she explained. "Mr. Jaragami has offered them very large sums of money to resettle in a different vicinity, and most of them have done so, but a few refuse to go. They claim this land is sacred to their ancestors. I'm afraid our country is steeped with these ignorant superstitions. Mr. Jaragami wishes to reach a compromise, so he has given them permission to stay here until the museum opens."

"What will happen then?" I asked.

"They will have to move."

"What if they don't want to?"

*Subject closed,* her tight smile said, so I didn't ask any more questions.

The gates slid open. The guard stepped aside. We drove up a long pathway lined with trees to the museum itself, an enormous white building lit by spotlights.

"It's beautiful," said Uncle Harvey. "Who's the architect?"

Meera said a name I didn't know, but Uncle Harvey seemed very impressed. The museum didn't look very beautiful to me; it was more like a building that had been blown up and put together by someone who'd lost the plans. Bits stuck out all over the place.

The museum had its own moat bisected by a long wooden bridge leading to the main entrance. We stepped out of the car. I looked down into the moat. Sprawled in the dust were three tigers. One of them twitched its tail and I jumped backwards.

Uncle Harvey was laughing at me. "You don't have to worry, Tom. They'll never climb up this."

"I'm not scared, Humperdinck. I was just surprised."

"If you ever call me that again . . ."

"Yes?"

"I don't know exactly what I'll do, but it will be very unpleasant."

"Okey-dokey. But can I ask you one question?"

"You can ask. I might not answer."

"Where did you get that middle name?"

"It was my father's idea of a joke."

"He gave you a middle name as a joke?"

"He thought it was funny. He was an idiot. You must have realized that by now."

When Grandpa died, he had barely been on speaking terms with either of his sons. Now I began to understand why. How could you choose your own son's name because you thought it was funny? It might bring a smile to your face for a day or two, but he'd have to live with it for the rest of his life. Suddenly my own dad didn't seem so bad after all.

"This way, please," said Meera.

She led us over the wooden bridge. The tigers were dozing under us. Their enclosure had steep sides, but no railings, no walls, no fence. One false step and you'd be slithering down the bank toward them. And was Uncle Harvey right? Were they really confined down there? Couldn't they scramble up the walls and get out? Meera didn't seem bothered, and she'd presumably been here hundreds of times before. We'd have to hope the tigers didn't jump that little bit higher just for us.

Meera led us into the museum's huge white entrance hall. Two massive portraits looked down on us from the ceiling, a pair of men standing side by side, their huge bodies and heads dominating the room. The first showed Tipu Sultan, dressed in a green jerkin and trousers, the material embroidered with diamonds and pearls. The other was of J.J., wearing his own ordinary clothes, jeans and sandals and a T-shirt that didn't look terribly clean. *We may be two hundred years apart,* the paintings seemed to be saying, *but we are brothers.*

The man himself was standing directly under his own portrait. In the time it had taken us to drive here through Bengaluru's traffic, he'd flown around the city and finished his meeting. As soon as he saw us, he called out, "Welcome to my museum. It is glorious, do you not agree?"

We agreed.

"I wish the public to see this," he said. "I wish them to understand the importance of this man to our nation, our national identity. They must know who he was and what he did, so they will never allow themselves to be conquered again. They will never permit a foreign invader to take control of our country. You see, my friends, we were ruled by you British for many years. I hope you will not mind me saying so, but we hated you very much. Nowadays, when India is so different, and Britain too, it is important to remember our histories."

"Of course it is," said my uncle. "I hope you'll also remember that the British brought some good things to India."

"Good things? You think so? Such as just what exactly?"

"The railways, for instance. And democracy."

"We would have built railways without you. As for democracy, I cannot give the British any credit for the creation of our democratic state, since they made so much effort to prevent it. Thankfully we are free of you today. We are our own masters. Look at us now. Look at me. My company is always in profit. We have six hundred thousand employees and an annual turnover of many billions of dollars. Do I need the British to help me?"

"I suppose not," said my uncle.

"Of course not. Now let us put our differences aside. Come and see my museum."

# 31

**J.J. walked us through** the rooms, talking constantly, explaining the purpose and provenance of different pictures or objects. I can't imagine why he was spending so much time with us. Perhaps he really did believe that we would be more likely to sell him the tiger if we thought it was going to a good home. *You can save your breath,* I wanted to say. But I held my tongue and nodded and smiled, trying to look interested as he bombarded us with information. Here was Tipu Sultan's favorite sword and there was a painting of his father. Here was a collection of coins from his treasury and a tent in which he once slept.

There were more tigers wherever we looked. They were engraved on the handle of a flintlock pistol, painted on the back of a helmet, woven into a carpet, decorating every available space.

A British soldier's uniform was on display, along with the weapons that he would have carried in the siege of Seringapatam: a musket, a bayonet, a dagger, a box of powder. They might have belonged to one of Horatio Trelawney's men, the soldiers who followed him up the walls and into the city, hacking their way through Tipu's army, heading for the palace and its treasures.

J.J. explained how he had acquired his collection. He hired two professors and thirty researchers. They hunted through the libraries, museums, and mansions of Britain, Europe, and America, following the trail of Tipu Sultan's belongings, bringing back to India all the objects that had been looted two hundred years ago.

Once the place was opened to the public, there would be guards in every room, watching the exhibits.

"We have no need for them now," said J.J. "The walls are enough to keep out unwelcome visitors."

"Don't you have alarms?" asked my uncle.

"Yes, of course. There are motion sensors in every room and alarms on all the doors and windows. But you don't have to worry—burglars won't even reach this part of the museum. There are high walls surrounding us. If someone did climb over them, which is most unlikely, they would be seen by the guards. If they got past the guards, which is even more unlikely, I have my secret weapon. You saw my babies on your way in?"

"The tigers?" asked Uncle Harvey. "They're magnificent."

"Thank you. They are also the most perfect guards. Every thief for miles around knows about my tigers. They have heard what happens to any robber who is caught in this museum."

"What does happen?" I asked.

J.J. grinned at me. "They become tiger food."

"You feed burglars to the tigers?"

"That is correct."

"Are you allowed to do that?"

"It is not strictly legal, but the police are not complaining. One less robber is one less problem for themselves." He watched our faces for a few moments, then burst out laughing. "Don't worry! Don't worry! I'm only joking. The tigers are for show, nothing more."

Still chuckling, he led us into the heart of the museum, a vast, airy room, its walls hung with big paintings in gilt frames and ceremonial swords in scabbards dangling with golden braids. Glass cases held coins, daggers, and a scepter.

And there was the throne, just as it had looked in the video, scarlet and gold, eight spears standing around the back, seven occupied, the eighth empty, awaiting its tiger.

Two men were standing beside the throne, one white, the other Indian. They came forward to meet us.

"May I introduce Mohibbul Nagra," said J.J. "He is the curator of my museum. This is Professor Timothy Watkins, a world expert on Tipu Sultan, who is currently consulting our archives. He has kindly agreed to lend his expertise today."

They shook hands with my uncle and said how pleased they were to meet him. No one took any notice of me.

J.J. said, "Now, please, will you allow Professor Watkins and Mr. Nagra to have a look at the tiger? If all is well, they will confirm its authenticity."

My uncle turned his attention to the experts. "What kind of tests do you want to do? I'm not happy for the piece to be manipulated or damaged in any way."

"You don't have to worry," said Professor Watkins. "We'll simply use our eyes. Mohibbul and I have many years of experience in identifying and classifying the works of this period. I can recognize a forgery without the need for tests. I do have one question, though. I'm fascinated to know how the tiger came into your possession."

"It's a long story," said Uncle Harvey. "But I'll give you the short version." He repeated the same tale that we'd told J.J.

Professor Watkins asked a few questions, but didn't seem to doubt a word. Then he said, "Could I see the tiger?"

"That's why I'm here." Uncle Harvey unzipped his bag.

The professor and the curator huddled together. They took turns holding the tiger, inspecting it from every angle, and talked in hushed tones. I couldn't hear what they were saying, but I searched their faces for clues.

J.J. didn't have much patience. He gave them about five minutes, then demanded to know what they'd decided. "What is your verdict, gentlemen? Is this the genuine article?"

"I'm a scientist," said Professor Watkins. "I can't give you any guarantees until I've seen the results of more detailed tests. But I would be astonished if they didn't confirm our intuitions. This is the one."

The curator added his voice to the chorus. "It is the real

thing, Mr. Jaragami. I'm sure it is. We have finally found the missing tiger."

"That's excellent." J.J. was beaming. "Thank you so much."

The professor and the curator knew they had been dismissed. They returned the tiger to my uncle and headed for the door.

When they had gone, J.J. turned to us with a huge smile. "So, to business. Let us not beat about the bushes. I wish to buy your tiger, Mr. Trelawney, and you wish to sell. Shall we make a deal?"

"I hope we can," said Uncle Harvey.

"I hope so too," said J.J. "What is your price?"

Uncle Harvey must have prepared himself for this moment. He would have rehearsed it in his mind, going over and over the best words to use, the price where he would begin, the price at which he would be willing to end. But he never got a chance to say anything, because I jumped in before him.

"Marko," I said.

# 32

***J.J. stared at me.*** He didn't say anything for a moment. Then he asked, "You are talking about this Marko again?"

"Yes."

"Why?"

"That's our price."

"I don't understand."

"We'll give you the tiger if you give us Marko."

"Marko, Marko—who is this Marko that you keep talking about?"

"He's the guy you hired to kill my grandfather."

That was when everyone started shouting at once. My uncle told me to calm down and J.J. said he didn't know who I was talking about. Two of the advisors jumped in as well, although I'm not actually sure what either of them was saying. I didn't say a word. I just stood there smiling. I didn't care how much they shouted at me. I just wanted to find the man who killed Grandpa.

When the shouting stopped, I repeated my offer. "You can have the tiger if you hand over Marko to the police. But you also have to get him to confess. There's no point in them arresting him if he denies what he's done."

"This person, this Marko," said J.J. "Who is he? Why do you think I have anything to do with him?"

"Oh, come on. You don't have to keep pretending you don't know him."

"I am not pretending. I really don't know him."

"He knows you."

"Many people know me. I do not know all of them. What does he say about me, this Marko? What has he been telling you?"

My uncle stepped in. "Wait a minute. Let's all calm down. Marko has nothing to do with the tiger. It's a separate issue and we'll deal with it later."

"No, we won't," I said.

"Tom—"

"He's a murderer. He killed Grandpa. You can't just let him get away with it." I turned from my uncle to J.J. "You told him what to do. You sent him to kill my grandfather. That makes you a murderer too."

The atmosphere in the room had changed. It was as if someone had opened a window and a chilly draft had blown past us all, sending a shiver up our spines. Smiles had gone from faces. Everyone was looking serious. J.J. was glaring at me as if I were an idiot, some little fool who had managed to sneak past his guards and get inside his private palace. He didn't appear to be frightened or even worried; he just looked cross.

"I want to do a deal with you," he said. "I will offer you a certain sum of money. You will want to earn more. I shall wish to pay less. We shall discuss the precise amount and, I hope, come to an agreement which is acceptable to us all. This is business. If you do not wish to do this—if you wish to make accusations and talk nonsense—then you are welcome to do so, but, please, not here. Not with me. I am too busy for such games. I have people waiting to see me. There you have it, Mr. Trelawney. The situation is not complicated. Do you want to deal with me or not? Yes or no?"

I managed to answer before my uncle. "Yes," I said. "But I've told you already, we don't want money. We want Marko."

"You don't want to sell the tiger?"

"No."

J.J. looked at my uncle. "He is talking for you both?"

"Not exactly."

"I thought not. Because he looks quite small to be in charge."

"He is younger than me, yes, but we're a team, him and me. We work together."

"So he speaks for you?"

Uncle Harvey hesitated. I could imagine what he was thinking. He wanted the money. He *needed* the money. But he cared about his father, too, and he wanted to catch his father's killer, just as I did. "Can I have a moment to talk to my nephew?"

"Of course you can." J.J. spoke to one of his assistants in a low tone. She answered him. Another of them stepped in. I wished I could speak their language. They talked for a minute or two, and then J.J. turned back to us. "We will talk tomorrow," he said. "Meera will call you in the morning. I am busy with meetings, but you can negotiate with her. She speaks for me. I hope we manage to reach an agreement. Goodbye, Tom. Goodbye, Harvey. It has been very interesting to meet you both."

# 33

**Meera escorted us out** of the museum. I was worried my uncle would double back and say we've changed our minds, here's your dumb tiger, give us the cash, but he stuck with me.

Meera said goodbye at the museum's entrance. Uncle Harvey gave her his card and told her the name of a hotel where we would probably be staying. It was where he always stayed when he was in Bangalore, he said. She tucked the card carefully into her purse and promised to call him in the morning. Then she folded her arms and waited for us to leave.

Uncle Harvey and I walked across the moat. Searchlights illuminated the enclosure below us. The three tigers were pacing silently back and forth.

My uncle said, "What's up, pussycat?"

The nearest tiger glared at him for a few seconds, as if it were measuring the distance between us, then dipped its head and continued padding around its drab home.

The black limousine was still waiting outside the museum, but its doors stayed firmly shut and the driver didn't even glance in our direction. We'd have to find our own way home.

We walked along the driveway toward the gates. I could see the guard in his uniform, standing under a spotlight, waiting for us. From here he looked like a toy soldier.

Uncle Harvey's voice came out of the gloom. "Tom?"

"Yes?"

"Do you want to tell me what that was all about?"

"I'm sorry I didn't tell you before," I said. "But I couldn't. I knew you'd try to stop me."

"You owe me a lot of money."

"You mean for the flights?"

"I mean the money I would have got from J.J. The money that would have paid off my debts. The money that would have saved me from getting two broken legs. Did you think I was joking around?"

"No, but—"

"I've got to get the money by the end of next week or he's going to break my legs. Do you understand what that means?"

"Yes, but—"

"We were this close to walking away with two million dollars. All my problems would have been solved. And you had to screw it up. I hope you're feeling pleased with yourself."

"Don't you care about catching the guy who killed Grandpa?"

"Of course I do. But I can't believe J.J. had anything to do with it. Marko looked to me like a loner. If he really killed Grandpa, he wasn't following orders."

"What do you mean, *if* he killed Grandpa? He told me he did."

"Like I said before, he might have been lying. Trying to scare you."

"He wasn't lying. He killed him. Now you just blew our one chance to catch him."

"I don't want to sound callous," said Uncle Harvey. "But Grandpa's dead. I care about my legs. And I'm a bit worried you might have blown my one chance to save them."

I thought about that for a moment. Then I said I was sorry.

"So am I," said Uncle Harvey. "I'm quite attached to my legs. I'm not looking forward to having them broken."

"Couldn't you borrow some money?"

"No one will lend me anything. I've already tried everyone I know."

I had thought I was being clever. I thought I'd thought of the perfect way to take my revenge on Marko and force him to face justice. Now I began to feel quite stupid. Was Uncle Harvey right? Had I messed everything up?

"We've still got the tiger," I said. "If you sold that, wouldn't you make enough money to stop them from breaking your legs?"

"I hope so. I'll let J.J. calm down overnight, then ring him in the morning."

"Are you going to sell it to *him?*"

"Who else? I'm sorry, Tom. I know you want revenge for Grandpa, and maybe we'll find a way to do it, but it's not going to happen right now. I need that money."

The guard opened the gate for us. We wished him good night and walked down the dark street that ran alongside the museum's high walls.

There were no streetlamps and the only light came from a few flickering lanterns in the village. Someone from there must have seen us, or been watching from the moment that we walked out of the gate, because he came running through the darkness toward us. As he came closer, I saw he was just a kid, smaller than me and skinnier, too.

"Money," he said. "Money."

If he'd been bigger, I would have thought he was mugging us. He looked hungry.

"Sorry," said my uncle. "I don't have any cash."

"Please give him something," I said.

Uncle Harvey stared at me. "What?"

"Just a few coins."

"You've just cost me a million dollars. Now you want me to give what little money I've got to a kid I don't know?"

"Yes."

"Fine. Whatever."

Uncle Harvey opened his wallet and handed over a note.

The boy wrapped his fingers around the money. "Thank

you," he said, addressing me rather than my uncle. He knew who had really given him the money. "You are from which country?"

"The U.S."

"Why are you here? Where do you go?"

"We've been in the museum and now we want to find a taxi. We need to get back to the center. Do you know where we should go?"

"Come with me. This way."

He gestured into the dark woods. I glanced at my uncle. Should we really dive in there, away from the light, away from the road, into the darkness, following a kid who we didn't know?

My uncle shrugged his shoulders. "Lead the way."

The boy led us into the woods. He told us his name. It sounded like "Methi," although I couldn't be sure; when I asked him to spell it, he just laughed. He didn't know how to spell in his own language, he explained, let alone ours. So we called him Methi.

As we walked through the dark woods, he chatted to us, asking our business, but he soon saw that we didn't want to tell him. So he told us his own story instead.

He had been born right here on this land, the same place that his family had lived for generations. Two years ago, a group of men arrived and announced that the land had been bought for development. They wouldn't say who had bought it or why. That didn't matter, they said. But you can no longer live here. You must move. We will pay you to go away.

Some of the villagers took the money and bought themselves plots of land in another village, thirty miles outside the city, but Methi's mother and father refused to move. This was their land, they insisted. *Our parents had lived here, our grandparents too, and we aren't going to leave, no matter how much we're offered.*

I asked Methi what he thought of their decision—what would he have done? Taken the money? Or stayed?—but I couldn't get him to understand my questions.

Architects and engineers came next, he said, taking photographs and surveying the land. Then the builders arrived. Huge machines ripped down trees and tore up the earth.

The villagers had watched the digging of the foundations, the construction of the walls, the arrival of trucks delivering great slabs of marble and sheets of glass.

Now the museum was almost finished and their shacks were clinging to this high wall. Methi didn't know how much longer he and his family would be here or when the order would come for them to be moved. Until then, they lived alongside the billionaire's museum, watching the artwork arriving, the security guards pacing around the walls, the helicopter flying in and out, bringing J.J. to inspect his most prized possessions.

"What about the tigers?" I asked. "Have you seen them?"

Through the gloom, I could just make out the big smile

on Methi's face. "The tigers are very good," he said. "I love the tigers! They are my good friends."

"How do you get to see them? Do you climb up and look over the wall?"

He laughed again. He and his friends didn't worry about walls or guards, he explained. When they wanted to see the tigers, they got a lift on one of the trucks driving through the gates and up to the museum. A man arrived every morning with fresh meat to feed the tigers. Methi and his friends sprang aboard as the trucks drove past, then rode them inside.

"Don't you get caught?" I asked.

"Yes."

"Then what happens?"

"They beat us," he said. "Here, see."

He pulled up his shirt to show me his scars. I could just barely see the welts crisscrossing his skin. He told me that his wrist had been broken by one of the guards and hadn't healed properly, so the bones were still wonky. But he didn't seem to care about any of this damage, as if getting beaten every now and then was just what you had to pay to see the tigers.

Soon we saw some lights glinting on the horizon. As we came closer, we saw they were the headlamps of cars on a main road. That was where Methi said goodbye and we waved down a cab. Methi didn't ask for any more money, but my uncle gave him another bill anyway.

The taxi drove us to the center of Bangalore and delivered us to a slightly rundown hotel where Uncle Harvey had stayed when he was last in the city.

The clerk jotted down the details of our passports, took Uncle Harvey's credit card details, and gave us a key for a room on the ninth floor. The elevator shuddered upward. Not everything in Bangalore was as smart and modern as J.J.'s tower.

The room itself was small and grubby. The window looked out at the ninth floor of other tower blocks. Uncle Harvey bolted the door and propped a chair against the handle. "Better safe than sorry," he said. "Now, which side of the bed do you want?"

We'd paid for two twin beds, but the clerk had given us a double. I chose the side nearest the window.

"We'll get it changed tomorrow," said my uncle. "You don't mind sharing for one night, do you? I don't snore."

He was lying. He fell asleep almost as soon as we got into bed and his snores kept me awake for a long time. I lay beside him, listening to the extraordinary noises coming out of his nose, the rattles and snuffles and snorts, and tried to decide what I would do in the morning when Uncle Harvey called Meera and offered to sell the tiger to J.J. for the bargain price of two million dollars. I knew he needed the money. I didn't want him to get two broken legs. But I wanted justice for Grandpa. Was there any way we could both get what we wanted?

# 34

**I woke up suddenly** and blinked into the darkness.

What was that? What had just woken me up?

Uncle Harvey?

He was lying beside me. Still fast asleep.

Had he been shouting in a dream? Or snoring again? Had he snored so loudly that I'd jolted awake? Could anyone make that much noise snoring?

Then I heard it again.

Someone was knocking on our door.

No, not knocking. Banging. Hammering. Throwing their whole weight against the panels.

That wasn't the sound of room service or the maid coming to change our sheets. That was someone trying to break down our door.

Who was it? J.J.? Had he come to steal our tiger? Or was it Marko? Would he kill us, wiping out the only people who could connect him to a murder?

I shouted a warning to my uncle. "Wake up! Wake up!"

"Huhhh?"

"Someone's breaking into our room."

Another crash. Heavier than the first.

Uncle Harvey was already scrambling out of bed. He yelled at me. "Open the window!"

*The window? Why the window?* But I didn't question him. I ran to the window and struggled with the lock. I yanked it. The window jerked upward. I thrust my head outside. It was a long drop down to the street. I turned my head to the left, then right, searching for a fire escape, a drainpipe, but there was nothing. No way down. Except jumping. And that wouldn't end well.

I turned around, wanting further instructions. Uncle Harvey had picked up a chair by two of its legs and now he was swinging it from side to side, testing its weight, ready to use it as a weapon.

"The window—" I said, but I didn't manage to speak another word before there was another crash and the door burst open.

A burly man stumbled into the middle of the room. He was wearing a uniform of brownish-khaki shirt and trousers, a thick belt pulled tightly around his waist, and heavy black boots. A beret was pulled down over his head. He looked like a Boy Scout. A tall, middle-aged Scout with a long wooden baton in his right hand, raised and ready to cause some serious damage. He saw me. His mouth opened. Then a chair hit him on the side of the head. He gave a low moan and fell to the floor.

A second man ran into the room. He was wearing the

same uniform as the first. My uncle swung at him, too, but this guy was prepared. He dodged backwards, reached down to his belt, and pulled out his own baton.

Uncle Harvey swung the chair back and forth, preparing to take another blow. For a moment, nothing happened. They faced off, the Boy Scout and my uncle, the baton and the chair, each waiting to see what the other was going to do. Then three more men came into the room. They screamed at us.

I didn't know what they were saying. I looked at my uncle. Should I jump out of the window?

No way. I didn't want to drop nine floors. I'd slither a floor or two, then drop the rest of the way.

My uncle was swinging the chair aggressively in front of him. I wished I had some kind of weapon too. There was nothing useful within reach.

One of the soldiers stepped toward me. He lifted his baton and lunged. I dodged. He swung again. I darted backwards. The window was right behind me. I didn't want to fall out. I shimmied one way, then the other. The soldier swung wildly at me, once, twice, then connected the third time and thwacked my shoulder with unbelievable force. I heard the thud before I felt the pain. Then I couldn't think of anything except the agony shuddering through my bones. I doubled over. The soldier hit me again. I slumped to the floor.

I got a glimpse of my uncle. He'd been surrounded by two more men. He got one of them in the belly with the chair. Then the other hit him in the face. Uncle Harvey collapsed against the wall, clutching his jaw with both hands.

I tried to get to my feet and help him, but the soldier kicked me in the stomach. I gasped and fell down. He kicked me again. I rolled over, trying to get away from his boots, and found myself face-to-face with my uncle. His cheek had been split open. Blood was dribbling through his nostrils and out of his lips. Even so, he managed to keep control of himself and say in a surprisingly calm voice, "What's going on? Why are you arresting us?"

That was when I realized these men were the police.

What were they doing here?

Oh.

Of course.

They'd come to find the boy who burned down their temple.

How had they traced me here?

Someone must have seen a suspicious foreigner lurking near the source of the fire. The old man, maybe. Or Ram. Or even Suresh. He thought he'd made a new friend, a foreigner. Then he put two and two together and realized I was the one who'd destroyed his temple and ruined his mom's chances of getting better.

# 35

***The room went quiet*** as a guy in a suit stepped through the doorway. From the way the others looked at him, I knew he was in charge.

He nodded to my uncle. "You are Mr. Harvey Trelawney?"

"Yes."

"And he is Mr. Tom Trelawney?"

"That's us. What's going on? Why did you smash down our door?"

"You were resisting arrest."

"No, we weren't."

"You did not open the door. You refused to let my men inside."

"They didn't even knock!"

"Of course they did, sir. They knocked several times and requested entrance. You did not answer."

"That's ridiculous! They just smashed the door down! If they'd knocked and said they were the police, we would have opened the door at once. And why did your man hit my nephew? What's wrong with you people? You can't just go around beating up children!"

"Please, sir, not to be shouting. If you will calm down, I will explain everything."

"You'd better," said Uncle Harvey. "You can't just break down the door of our hotel room. I'm going to ring the front desk and tell them what's going on."

"Don't worry about the front desk, sir. They are perfectly aware of the situation."

"Oh, are they? Terrific. Could you explain it to me too, please?"

"Of course, sir. Right away. Please, you will put on some clothes. Then we will take the chance to talk."

My uncle nodded to me. We both got dressed. I turned my back on the cops to pull on my pants. As I was turning around again, I cupped my phone from the bedside table and slid it into my pocket. No one saw me. That was good. In a minute, I'd say I needed the bathroom. Then I'd call Mom or Dad and ask them to call . . . Who could they call? Not the police. So who else? A lawyer. That's what I needed. A good lawyer. Someone who spoke the local language. Would Mom and Dad agree to pay for a lawyer? They'd have to. Otherwise they wouldn't be seeing me for a long, long time.

Uncle Harvey sat down on the bed. He mopped his face with the corner of a sheet, leaving a long smear of fresh blood.

I wanted to talk to him. I wanted to ask his advice. Should

I act like a tough guy in a movie and refuse to speak a word till my lawyer arrived? Or confess immediately?

I didn't have much experience with the police, but I had been hauled before Authority often in the past. Authority with a capital *A* came in many forms: my mom, my dad, my teachers, the principal, even a social worker once. All of them had called me before them and asked me to explain myself, justify myself, come clean about my crimes.

Confess or deny, that's your choice in such a situation, and I still wasn't sure of the best strategy.

Confession can sometimes lead to a lesser punishment.

Denial only works if there's no actual evidence linking you to the crime.

Which would my uncle choose?

He'd deny everything. I was sure he would. Confession wasn't his style.

What if I'd left fingerprints? What if they had a statement from Ram or Suresh or someone else who had seen me in the temple? Shouldn't I confess everything right away?

"We have had a complaint," said the policeman. Looking at him, I'd never have guessed that's what he was. His face was plump and comfortable, the cheery features of a butcher or a baker, the type of man who couldn't resist sampling his own products during quiet moments in the shop. "We would like to ask you a few questions. Would you mind?"

"Not at all," said my uncle.

"Thank you. It won't take very long. May I first make sure of some details? Your name is Harvey Trelawney?"

"That's correct."

"You arrived in this country when?"

"A couple of days ago."

"And the purpose of your visit?"

"Business and pleasure. I have a client here, but I've also brought my nephew on his first trip to India." He was just about to explain further when he noticed what was happening on the other side of the room. "Hey! What are they doing?"

Three policemen were searching my uncle's bag. They'd tipped the contents on the floor and were sorting through his things, running their fingers along the seams of his trousers, opening his paired socks, rifling through the pages of his books.

What if one of them found the tiger?

I glanced at my uncle. The same thought had obviously occurred to him. He was standing up, his face red. "You can't do that! Put that down! Get out of my bag!"

"You do not have worry," said the policeman. "It is only a precaution."

"Do you have a warrant?"

"This is not your country, sir. The situation is different here. We have no need of a warrant."

"Where's my phone? I'm calling my lawyer. I'm calling the embassy. You're going to regret this." Uncle Harvey leaned over to his bedside and scrabbled for his phone.

A shout came from the other side of the room. Everyone turned to look. One of the policemen was holding up two small plastic bags stuffed with tiny white pills. My first thought was relief: at least they hadn't found the tiger. Then I realized what the pills must be. The police wouldn't be interested in aspirin. They'd found drugs.

The room's attention turned back to Uncle Harvey.

"They're not mine," he said.

"They are in your bag," replied the cop.

"I didn't put them there."

"Then who did?"

"You tell me."

The plainclothes officer gave an order to his subordinate, who brought the drugs to him. He opened one bag and dipped his forefinger into the contents, rummaging through the pills. Then he lifted his head and looked sternly at my uncle. "For this quantity, even if you find the best lawyer in India, I would estimate eight to ten years in a high-security prison."

"That's ridiculous. They're not mine."

"It would be very much easier for everyone if you would tell the truth."

"I am telling the truth. They are not mine."

"I've seen your record, Mr. Trelawney. You spent three months in prison in Goa and only escaped a much longer sentence on a technicality. You had a good lawyer on that occasion. This time, you will need an even better one."

"That was nothing to do with drugs," protested my uncle. "If you've really read the records, you'll know I shouldn't have been in prison at all."

The policeman ignored him and issued another order. His men came forward. One of them pocketed my uncle's phone.

"Where are you taking us?" asked my uncle.

No one answered.

"I want to make a phone call," he insisted. "I want to speak to the American embassy."

No one took any notice of him. No one seemed to care. Without a word, a uniformed policeman yanked Uncle Harvey's hands behind his back and clipped cuffs over his wrists. A cop shoved my shoulder. They didn't bother handcuffing me; I suppose they thought I wasn't worth the trouble.

They marched us to the door.

"What about my stuff?" said Uncle Harvey. "What's going to happen to my bag?"

The only answer he got was another push.

I wanted to know the answer to that too. What would they do with his bag? And, much more important, what would happen to the tiger? What would the police think when they went through his belongings and found it? Would they assume it was just a cheap fake, a piece of junk we'd picked up for a few rupees? Would they give it back to us when we were released?

I glanced back at the two bags of drugs, which the policeman had put on the bed, and I had a sudden, terrible thought.

What if they *were* my uncle's?

What if he'd been carrying those pills in his bag all the

time, taking them to Ireland for his dad's funeral, then bringing them to India?

Could he have done that?

No, no, no. My uncle might have been many things, but he wasn't an idiot. He would never have been so stupid.

Would he?

# 36

**Downstairs in the lobby,** guests craned their necks to watch our progress. Some of them were wearing pajamas. What time was it? Three in the morning? Four? Five? Six? Why were so many people awake in the middle of the night? Had they gotten out of bed especially to come and watch us being arrested?

If things had been different, I would have winked and waved at the crowd. Maybe even signed some autographs. But my shoulder was still hurting, and my ribs, too, and I was feeling too scared about what might happen next. I couldn't even imagine where they were taking us. I'd seen a movie about a guy in an Indian prison, and it hadn't looked nice. I remembered the walls dripping with slime, the police inspector flexing his arms, punching the prisoners.

Someone shouted my name. "Mr. Trelawney! Mr. Trelawney!"

I looked around to see who was shouting at me.

It was the receptionist. She was running after us, waving

a bill. She wasn't interested in me; she wanted some money from my uncle.

He hadn't even turned to look at her. I suppose he had more important things to worry about.

I was just mouthing "Sorry" to the receptionist when I saw Marko.

Standing in the crowd. Watching us. Smiling.

When he realized I'd seen him, he didn't bother hiding. His smile broadened and he lifted his arm and waved.

I seethed with rage. I wanted to punch him. I wanted to claw my way through the crowd and hurl myself at him and knock him to the ground and kick his head in.

But I was jerked forward by one of the policemen, led across the lobby, and taken through the door.

Him. Here.

Marko.

That explained everything!

Our arrest had nothing to do with the temple or the fire. And the drugs definitely weren't my uncle's.

It was all about the tiger.

Now that we were out of the way, Marko just had to saunter upstairs, rummage through my uncle's bag, and take what he wanted.

How had Marko found us? How did he know we were here? How did he get the police to do his dirty work for him?

He could have followed us from the museum to the road,

picked up another taxi and driven behind us to this hotel. We never looked over our shoulders. It hadn't even occurred to us that we were being followed. Then he would have summoned some crooked cops and ordered them to arrest us. I'd already seen the way things worked here. If you had a bit of cash, you could bend the law, get the authorities to do what you wanted.

I had to tell my uncle what I'd seen.

Not yet. Not now. He was three steps ahead of me with a burly policeman standing on either side of him. They were treating us like major criminal suspects, as if he were a terrorist or a bank robber and I was his accomplice.

My uncle was used to this. He'd been in prison before. He knew what to do. How to talk to the police. How to negotiate. What to say, what not to say.

But I didn't have a clue.

I was just a kid. Sure, I'd been in trouble before, but nothing like this.

What was I going to do? How could I get home?

I still had my phone in my pocket, but I didn't want to pull it out now. They'd confiscate it right away. I'd have to wait. Then I'd call Mom and Dad and beg them to come and get me.

Three police cars were parked directly outside the hotel. The sky was pale. It must have been just before dawn. The street was already packed with people. A line of uniformed officers kept back the crowds.

Like in a movie, the policeman held the top of my head

before pushing me down and into the back of the car. They took Uncle Harvey around to the other side and shoved him in too.

Doors slammed. The engine roared.

Sirens blaring, we sped away from the hotel and into the crowded streets, cars and rickshaws bumping onto the curb to let us past.

We had an escort, a car behind us and a car ahead. People peered at the car, trying to see through the windows, probably wondering who we were.

My uncle turned to me. "We've been in this country for three days now and finally we've found a way to defeat the traffic."

I could see fresh blood bubbling from his nostrils, but he was grinning as if he'd never had more fun in his life.

"I saw Marko," I said.

The smile left his face. "Where?"

"In the hotel."

"What was he doing?"

"Nothing. Just watching. But he was smiling."

"Marko." Uncle Harvey shook his head and swore violently several times. Then he glanced at me. "Sorry."

"Don't worry. I've heard it all before."

"So. Marko. He set it up."

"How did he know where we were?"

"I suppose J.J. told him."

"Do you think they work together?"

"I think he works for J.J.," said Uncle Harvey. "They must

have been in this together from the beginning. That would explain how the cops got involved so quickly. I don't know if Marko could have arranged all this on his own."

"Why would J.J. do this?"

"To save himself a couple million dollars."

"He's a billionaire. Why would he care about two million dollars?"

"Maybe it's not the money. Maybe he's just desperate to get his hands on the tiger. Maybe you panicked him."

"Me? How?"

"You said you'd only give him the tiger in exchange for Marko. If he really was involved in Dad's death, he couldn't give you Marko, so he wouldn't be able to get the tiger. He must have been worried we'd never sell it to him. So he decided he had to steal it instead."

I thought about that for a moment. It didn't sound good. If it was just us against Marko, I could imagine how we might be able to get out of this tricky situation. But us against J.J. and all the power that his money would be able to buy—how could we possibly win?

My uncle must have been able to see how worried I was feeling. "Don't panic," he said. "You'll be fine. You won't go to prison."

"Why not?"

"Because you're young. And foreign. They won't want to lock you up. It would be an international embarrassment. They'll ask you some questions, then put you on the first plane back to New York."

"What if they found out about the fire?"

"Which fire?"

"In the temple."

"They'll never connect you to that. Don't worry. You're going to be fine."

"What about you?"

"I imagine they'll give me ten years."

"But they can't! You didn't do anything."

"They found those drugs in my bag."

"That's so unfair!"

Uncle Harvey shrugged his shoulders, then winced. He must have been aching from the beating. "They can do what they want. It's their country." Then he smiled. "But like I said, you don't have to worry. You're going to be fine. You'll be home in a couple of days. I can just see your dad's face when he hears I've been locked up. He'll think I've got exactly what I deserve."

I wanted to smile back and show that, just like him, I could laugh in the face of danger, but I didn't feel much like smiling. My shoulder and ribs still hurt. And I was worried. Being caught with drugs—that's no joke. Would I really be sent home? What if I wasn't? Would Mom and Dad come and rescue me?

I could imagine them visiting me in my cell and shaking their heads and saying, *Oh, Tom,* in that despairing tone of voice that I knew so well.

*Oh, Tom. What's wrong with you?*

I had a sudden thought.

I whispered, "I've got my phone."

"Where?" Uncle Harvey whispered back.

"In my pocket. And my hands are free. Should I call someone?"

"Yes."

"Who?"

"I don't know. Let me think."

"I could call my mom," I said.

"Why not? She'll be able to help us. Wait! You won't have long," whispered my uncle. "They'll take away the phone as soon as they realize what you're doing. Do you understand?"

"Yes."

"So you have to be quick. Don't waste time. Yes?"

"Yes."

"Tell her she has to ring the embassy. There won't be one in Bangalore, but she should ring the embassy in Delhi. She has to tell them how old you are. She has to make them—"

The rest of his words were cut off by a loud bang.

The car swerved. We were thrown sideways.

Another bang, even louder.

I was hurled backwards.

Our car skidded to a halt.

The road was littered with broken glass. The traffic had come to a halt. Drivers had sprung out of their cars. Now they were shouting and waving their arms. Through the windshield of a small green car, I could see a man slumped over the steering wheel.

A woman was climbing out of the crushed back door, clutching her eyes. Blood seeped between her fingers.

The car ahead of us, the first in our convoy, had been racing along the road, swerving around buses and between rickshaws, clearing a path for us. This strategy had been working very well until a small green car had either failed to get out of the way or, more likely, tried to take advantage of the space that had opened up to let us through.

I heard a shout. Then a scream.

A fight had broken out. The driver of the green car had staggered from the wreckage and thrown himself at the police, who he must have blamed for hitting him.

Four of them had been riding in the car that hit him, and all four fought back immediately. They were armed with batons and pistols, but they didn't need their weapons. They simply knocked him to the ground with their fists, then kicked him with their shiny black boots.

That should be have been the end of the fight, and would have been if his wife hadn't joined in, blood still streaming from her eyes. She charged forward and sprang onto the back of the nearest policeman.

Another woman emerged from the car and joined in.

The police still would have won easily if several onlookers hadn't chosen to get involved. I can't imagine why they did. They must have known they'd only get hurt.

The car behind us held four more police. Now they joined in too. One pulled his baton from his belt and rained down blows on the heads and backs of anyone within reach. Another pointed his pistol into the air and fired a shot.

The noise must have been intended to quiet the crowd and persuade them to go away, and it worked with some of them, but enraged others, bringing them out of their cars and into the fight.

Soon the police were lost under a storm of fists and feet.

Our driver and his passenger hesitated for a moment, glancing at us, then the fight. Then they opened their doors and ran to help their comrades.

"Tom," hissed my uncle.

"Yes?"

"This is your chance. Run."

"But what will—?"

"Just run," interrupted my uncle. "Then ring the embassy. Someone will come and find you. They'll get you home."

"What about you?"

He nodded at his wrists. One end of the handcuffs was still attached to him, but the other had been clipped around the inside door handle. With a chisel or a screwdriver, we could have freed him in a moment, but we didn't have either.

"What will you do?" I asked.

"Don't worry about me," he said. "I'll be fine."

"But what if they—"

"I told you, I'll be fine. You're wasting time, Tom. Get out of here. Go on. Run."

I hated the idea of leaving him there, but I knew he was right. I had to take my chance. I wouldn't get another.

Then I looked at the front seat. And knew what I had to do.

I opened my door and jumped out of the car.

My feet crunched on broken glass. A man barged past me, fists flailing, and threw himself into the fight that was still raging.

The police were outnumbered, but battling hard, crunching their batons into knees and noses. None of them noticed me. They had more important things taking up their attention.

I slid into the front seat of our police car, slammed the door after me and turned the key in the ignition.

# 37

***I'd only driven a car*** once before. That had been in Peru, earlier in the year, and Uncle Harvey had been sitting beside me, giving me instructions. This time he was in the back, but it didn't matter. I didn't need his help. I could remember what to do. Driving isn't difficult. You just have to keep your foot down and avoid hitting anything.

That was the only tricky bit.

I hit a lot of stuff.

Some people, too.

The first was our driver. The car rammed into the back of his knees, sending him flying.

I didn't care about him. He and his friends had just beat up me and my uncle, and I was sure he would have been happy to run me down too. But I felt bad about the rickshaw that I knocked over next, spilling its occupants onto the pavement. I wanted to stop and see if they were OK, but I knew I had to keep driving. The police were already charging after us.

I wrenched the wheel. The car rammed into a truck and bounced aside.

Uncle Harvey was yelling at me from the back seat, but I couldn't hear what he was saying and didn't have time to ask him to clarify.

The side of a bus loomed up ahead of me. I wrestled with the steering wheel. We swerved to the right. People threw themselves out of the way.

A bicycle crashed into the windshield. Where did that come from? Cracks wriggled across the glass. Had I killed the cyclist? No sign of him. No sign of blood, either. I hope he was OK. Would the windshield collapse on me? No time to worry about that now. Faster, faster. Down here. Up there. Through that gap. What's that? I could see a blur of other cars and trucks heading toward me. I was on the wrong side of the road. How? Who knows! I couldn't get out of their way, so I just drove straight ahead and hoped they would get out of mine.

*Bang!* A car clipped us. Metal screeched. I saw a face, the driver, his eyes wide open, his mouth, too, and then he was gone.

My uncle was still shouting at me from the back seat. But I had more important things to worry about.

*Crash!* A truck crunched against our flank. The mirror disappeared, leaving nothing but a sprig of trailing wires.

My window was open. How did that happen? Oh, yes. The glass had been knocked out. All over my lap.

Two cars were coming toward me. There was no room to pass between them. I could hear their brakes screeching, but they weren't going to stop in time. Through the windshields I could see the drivers, their faces frozen with terror.

I yanked the steering wheel. The car swerved, skidded, bumped onto the pavement, and smashed through a market stall. Lemons cascaded onto the windshield. A watermelon crunched in half, spilling its insides. The world went red.

"Wipers!" yelled my uncle.

What did that mean?

Oh, right. Wipers.

How do they turn on?

Dunno.

No time to find out.

Didn't matter, anyway. The wind had already blown those scarlet chunks of watermelon from the windshield, clearing my view, and I could see the road ahead.

I rammed my foot on the accelerator and sent us through a gap in the traffic. Then I lost control of the car. We must have skidded. I don't know why. Suddenly we were on the other side of the road.

A brick wall.

Coming closer at unbelievable speed.

No time to think.

No time to move.

Straight into the side of a shop.

The noise!

My body snapped forward.

My head bounced off the edge of the steering wheel.

I died.

Oh, no. I hadn't. Dying wouldn't hurt so much. I had one blissful moment of peace, then the world returned with a vengeance, injecting pain into every corner in my body, and a voice was screaming in my ear, telling me to pick myself up and run.

No, thank you. I don't want to run. I like it here. I'm cozy.

"Run!" yelled the voice again.

I opened my eyes. I could see glass and bricks and blood and the face of a boy, not much younger than me, peering through what had once been a windshield. His mouth opened and strange sounds came out.

"Get out, you idiot! Get out and run!"

That wasn't the boy talking. That was my uncle. I turned around and looked at him slumped on the back seat. Blood was trickling down his face.

"Run!" he yelled for the hundredth time.

I heard my voice. It sounded very distant. "What about you?"

"Forget about me. Just go!"

I pushed the door. It sagged open. I stepped out. To my surprise, I could stand up without falling over. I didn't think my legs were going to work. I flexed my hands. They worked too. That was good news. Now what? Should I run? Could I? And where would I go?

The boy grinned at me. "You drive good!"

"Thanks."

"Which country are you from?"

"I can't remember."

He laughed.

You know what was really funny?

It was true.

If I'd sat down and thought about things, I probably could have remembered everything about myself and my life, but at this moment my mind felt empty. As if that crash had wiped me clean.

I heard a siren.

That brought me back to life, sparking ideas in parts of my brain that had previously gone dormant.

Time to move. Time to get out of here.

But not alone.

# 38

***I went around to my uncle's*** side of the car and opened his door.

The handle had broken off and was now joined to him and his handcuffs. He was still attached to a piece of the car, but free enough that he could walk.

We hobbled down the street.

At the corner, I looked back. The boy had been joined by a bunch of friends and all of them were scrambling over the police car, pulling it apart, taking pieces as souvenirs.

Uncle Harvey and I jogged down that street, then another. People stared at us. Of course they did. We were foreigners. Our faces were covered in blood. My uncle was wearing handcuffs. I'd have stared at us too.

"We've got to get off the street," I said to my uncle.

"I know. I know. I'm just trying to think where to go."

"How about a hotel?"

"I don't have any money."

"What about your credit card?"

"They got that, too. Along with everything else. I don't

know why they didn't just take the tiger and leave us the rest. Have you still got your phone?"

"Yes."

"Don't give it to me now. First we need to find ourselves somewhere to hide. Come on. Whatever you do, don't run. Just walk slowly and look as if everything's cool."

There was a building site on the other side of the street. One of these days it was going to be become a block of apartments, but right now it wasn't much more than the walls and the floors, the timbers exposed, the concrete unfinished. A wooden fence guarded it from the street. Uncle Harvey shoved his shoulder against the slats and made a gap big enough to get through. I clambered after him and pulled the fence shut again. Several people in the street must have seen us, but no one shouted at us and no one told us to get out. I hoped none of them were calling the police.

We climbed up two flights of stairs and found ourselves a nice clean patch of recently concreted floor.

"We'll stay here till the builders arrive," said Uncle Harvey. "Then we'll shove off and find somewhere else. Now give me the phone."

"Who are you going to call?"

"Just give it to me."

"Okey-dokey."

I handed over my phone. He rolled up his sleeve. A number was written on the skin just above his wrist. He tapped the number into my phone.

A moment later, I heard Tanya's voice yelling out of the

phone, asking what he thought he was doing, waking her up in the middle of the night.

He started explaining, but she ended the call.

Uncle Harvey was grinning.

"I'm in love," he said.

He called her again. This time he only managed to say, "Please don't hang up the phone" before she hung up.

He was still grinning. He called her once more and left a message. "I've got to talk to you," he said. "It's urgent. It really is. I'm sorry to be ringing you so early, but you'll understand why when you talk to me."

He ended the call, waited a minute, then rang her again.

"Please," he said. "Just listen to me for a minute." There was a pause. Then he said, "I'm on the run from the police, I need money, and you're the only person in the entire world who can help me." I heard laughter coming down the phone. "It's true," said Uncle Harvey. "I promise on my mother's life. Yes, you're right, she is. I promise on my own life, how about that? Just let me explain. It won't take long."

He was wrong. It took ages. He told her about the letters, the tigers, J.J., and the police. I did try to stop him, but he shook his head and gestured for me to shut up. I suppose he felt he had to be honest with her if she was going to help us, and maybe he was right.

She made him promise on his mother's grave that he was telling the truth.

Then she said she'd leave her hotel as soon as she was dressed and get on the first train to Bangalore.

Uncle Harvey switched off the phone. "If she's lucky with the trains, she'll be here in four or five hours."

"Then what will we do?"

"Borrow some money, buy a couple of new passports, and get the hell out of this country."

"How can you buy a passport?"

"You can buy anything if you have enough money. Like the visas, remember?"

"What about Marko?"

"Forget about Marko."

"You're just going to let him get away with it?"

"We don't have much choice."

"That's terrible!"

"Yup."

My uncle shrugged, then winced.

I felt furious. And miserable.

Marko had murdered my grandfather. Got the tiger. And earned two million dollars.

Game, set, and match.

I wanted to kill him. I couldn't understand why my uncle didn't feel the same. Yes, of course, he was worried about saving his own legs, but why wasn't he even more worried about locking up the man who murdered his dad? We couldn't let him get away with it. We just couldn't.

But what could we do? How could we stop him?

The police weren't going to help us. Neither would anyone else.

We'd messed up.

No, I'd messed up.

Uncle Harvey had been right. I should have kept my mouth shut. We should have sold the tiger to J.J., taken the money, then called the police and gotten them to deal with Marko. I don't know why I hadn't done that in the first place. What an idiot. Did I really think I could blackmail a billionaire? J.J. would never have done a deal with me. Of course he wouldn't. I'd been a fool. I should have let Uncle Harvey handle the whole thing. Then I could have gone home with a million dollars and tracked down Marko from the safety of my own home. I'd messed up everything.

Unless . . .

Would that work?

It might.

I spent a few minutes thinking it through, looking at my idea from every angle, trying to imagine how it would work and what might go wrong. Then decided I had no choice.

I told my uncle what I wanted to do.

He shook his head. "Don't be an idiot, Tom. Forget Marko. Forget the tiger. We're going to get out of India. We have to save our skins."

"What about your debts?"

"I'll find a way to pay them. I don't know how, but I'll think of something."

I thought about it for a moment. Then I nodded. "You leave India if you want to. But I'm going to break into the museum and steal J.J.'s tigers. Then he'll have to hand over Marko."

"And how exactly are you going to do that?"

"I'm not sure."

"You do know you'll never make it, don't you?"

"I don't see why not. I've broken into places before."

"Oh, yes? Like where?"

"My school."

"Your school," he said sarcastically.

"Yes."

"What did you do? Climb through the window?"

"Yes, I did, actually."

"Did your school have an alarm system?"

"No."

"Laser beams? Motion sensors? Armed guards?"

"No."

"I thought not. The museum does. Even if you manage to climb over the walls and evade the guards, you'll be confronted by an immensely sophisticated alarm system. Then there's the tigers, of course. You don't want to be eaten by them, do you?"

I shook my head.

I'd forgotten the tigers.

I remembered the way J.J. had laughed and said he was only joking about feeding thieves to them.

Had he been joking? Or was he telling the truth?

I didn't want to be tiger food.

Wait a minute.

What if . . .?

Yes.

I grinned.

"I've got it," I said.

"Got what?"

"I know how to get in there."

"Oh, yeah? How?"

I told him.

He listened in silence, then asked a couple of pertinent questions.

I could see him thinking.

Was he impressed by my guts? Or excited by the thought of all eight tigers sitting in the museum, waiting to be stolen? Did he think they'd make him enough money to pay off his debts?

Uncle Harvey said, "Is there any way I can stop you from doing this idiotic thing?"

"No."

"Then I'd better come with you."

"You don't have to."

"I know I don't. But I'm going to."

"Why?"

"Someone has to stop you from getting killed."

# 39

**I was impatient to get** moving, but we couldn't do anything till Tanya arrived, so we sat there, watching the sun rise slowly up the opposite wall. We were both too tired and thirsty to do anything else. The heat was intense. I did go on one exploratory expedition, padded up and down the stairs, hunting for water, but the plumbing hadn't been connected yet and every tap was dry.

We were lucky in one way. The builders never turned up, so we had the site to ourselves. We used a room on the ground floor as a toilet. Judging by the smell, we weren't the first.

There was no sign of the police, either. What would they be doing now? Searching our room in the hotel? Alerting the airport and the train station? Sending our pictures to the newspapers and the TV stations? Would the news cross the world? Would Mom and Dad glimpse my face on a TV screen? Or would they be called by Interpol, eager to know more information about my previous crimes, my state of mind, my psychological profile?

Just after midday, Tanya called my phone and said she was in a taxi driving through Bangalore. Uncle Harvey told her to dump that cab and pick up another, then come to our street. We'd spotted its name out of a window.

We snuck out of our comfy building site and walked down the street, keeping watch for cops. There didn't seem to be any around. Soon we came to a dingy alleyway between two tall buildings. We hid in there and Uncle Harvey texted Tanya from my phone, telling her how to find us.

Five minutes later, she appeared at the end of our alleyway, her slim body silhouetted against the sunlight. "Hello?" she called out. "Are you there?"

I've never been happier to see anyone in my life. Especially because she was carrying two big bottles of water.

She gave Uncle Harvey a long hug and me a shorter one. Then she handed over the bottles. Once we'd drunk enough, she said, "So what are we going to do now? You want me to smuggle you out of the country? Shall I take you home with me to Tel Aviv?"

"Yes, please," said Uncle Harvey. "But first I need to deal with these."

He raised his right hand and showed her the handcuffs.

"I saw a shop on my way in," she said. "He should be able to handle it."

She led us down the street to a tiny shop, more like a cubicle, where a man in a brown apron was cutting keys. For a hundred rupees, he clipped the cuffs from my uncle's wrists. For a hundred more, he promised to forget he'd ever seen us.

Two blocks away, we found a cheap hotel. Tanya went into the lobby alone and booked two rooms, then came to get us. The clerk gave us a quick glance, then returned his attention to the cricket on the TV. India was playing Australia. The crowd was roaring. Someone had just dropped a catch.

Our rooms were side by side on the first floor. I shut myself in the bathroom, stripped off my clothes, and inspected my body. I had some painful bruises along my ribs and several cuts on my arms, but they were already beginning to heal. I was going to be fine.

While Uncle Harvey and I were getting clean, Tanya went out and bought bandages, antiseptic cream, new clothes for both of us, and takeout from the curry house across the street. I couldn't quite understand why she was spending so much money on us. When I asked my uncle, he grinned and said, "It's very simple. She likes me."

We sat on the floor in their room, eating spicy vegetable curry and clammy rice out of little metal boxes, mopping up the gravy with flat brown pieces of bread that my uncle said were called parathas. It was the strangest breakfast I'd ever had, and one of the best.

"So what now?" said Tanya. "How am I going to get you out of here?"

"We have something we have to do first," I said.

"Oh, yes? What's that? Steal the Taj Mahal?"

"Good plan," said Uncle Harvey. "Will it fit in your backpack?"

"We can try."

They grinned at each other. Then Uncle Harvey explained what we were actually planning to do. "J.J. stole our tiger. We're going to get it back and take all seven of his, too."

We spent the entire day in that dingy little room. Tanya went out to buy more food and drink, but otherwise the three of us sat on the bed or paced back and forth across the floorboards, discussing what had been happening and what might happen next.

Tanya wanted to know about the Trelawneys. We told her some family history, then described our adventures together earlier in the year, explaining about John Drake's diaries and the *Golden Hind* and Otto Gonzalez and everything else that had happened in Peru.

In return, Tanya told us about her own life. She had been born in a small town in the very north of Israel, near enough to Lebanon that mortars and rockets sometimes landed in the streets. She went to school and university, did her military service, and now worked in a computer firm in Tel Aviv. This was her third visit to India and she'd traveled all over the country. Her flight home left next Wednesday. When Uncle Harvey invited her to come and stay with him in New York, she nodded seriously and said, "I would like that very much."

# 40

**My phone woke me** at five in the morning. I pulled on my clothes, tiptoed into the corridor, and knocked on their door. No answer. Uncle Harvey was meant to be up before me. Maybe he'd slept through his alarm. I knocked louder. A groan came from the other side. "Who's that?"

"Me."

Silence for a moment. Then my uncle's voice: "Five more minutes."

"We have to go."

"Give me five minutes."

"You have to get up."

Silence.

I rapped on the door with my knuckles. "Humperdinck! Come on, Humperdinck! It's time to get up! Humperdinck!"

I heard a thud. Footsteps. Then the door opened. He peered at me through half-closed eyes. "If you ever call me that again—"

"Please just get up. Get dressed. We have to go."

"Will you ever call me that again?"

"No."

"You promise?"

"I promise."

"Fine. Come in. I'll get dressed."

We went inside. I pulled the door shut after me and hoped I hadn't woken any curious fellow guests along the corridor. Tanya was sitting up in bed, a sheet wrapped around her body. She smiled. "Morning, Tom. Sleep well?"

"Yes, thanks."

"Do you want to come and have something to eat? There's a bit of food left from last night."

We ate a hurried breakfast of soggy parathas left out from last night's supper. Uncle Harvey grumbled about the lack of coffee. How was he supposed to commit a robbery, he said, if he hadn't even had a decent cup of coffee?

Tanya kissed me on the cheek and Uncle Harvey on the lips, then whispered, "Good luck. Be careful."

"We will," said my uncle. "Now go back to sleep. We'll be back before you wake up."

"I hope so."

We snuck out of the room. My uncle closed the door and hung a Do Not Disturb notice over the handle.

Downstairs in the lobby, the clerk was head down on the desk, fast asleep. He didn't even stir as we tiptoed past. Uncle Harvey unbolted the front door and we walked into the street.

It wasn't yet dawn, but Bengaluru was already full of noise. Shopkeepers were opening their shutters, and jammed buses were bringing workers into the city. A stall on the other side of the street was selling glasses of tea or coffee. I thought my uncle might try to delay our departure even longer, but he stepped straight into the street and waved at a taxi.

The drive took about an hour. We arrived in daylight. To my surprise, the driver didn't ask why we wanted to get out in the middle of the woods beside a half-built museum, just took my uncle's money and accelerated away.

We walked through the trees to the village. The houses looked as if they were held together with nothing more than mud and luck. A storm would have lifted the rickety roofs and whisked the walls away, leaving the villagers huddling on the ground, wrapped in their blankets.

The only sign of life was an old goat tethered to a stake stuck in the ground, nuzzling the earth with his rubbery lips.

We had almost reached the nearest house when three skinny teenagers strolled out of the village. I don't know if they'd been watching our approach or had just happened to walk past now, but they swaggered into the middle of the road and stared suspiciously at us as if they had been appointed to protect the village.

They were soon joined by another kid, then two more. Six against two. They blocked our way, their heads raised, their faces defiant. *This is our home,* their expressions said. *It might not look like much, but it's ours, and we don't like intruders.*

One of the kids raised his right hand, pointed at us, and yelled a few words, a short phrase. He must have been warning us. Telling us to turn around and go home.

He said the same words again. Now I realized he was speaking English.

"You must give me money!"

"Here you go." Uncle Harvey reached into his pocket and pulled out a crumpled bill. "Here's five hundred rupees."

All six kids ran forward, but my uncle raised his hand and held the money over their heads, the note flickering on the breeze like a worm on the end of a hook.

"I want to speak to Methi," he said. "Where's your friend Methi?"

Their faces were blank. They didn't know what he was talking about. One of them tried jumping higher for the money and another wandered a few paces away, bored or distrustful. My uncle didn't give up. "Methi," he said. "He's a boy who lives in this village. His name is something like Methi. Come on, you must know him. Methi. Mathi. Mothy. Murphy."

Finally one of them answered. "Methi?"

"Yes! Methi! Where is he?"

"Methi! Methi!" They were all laughing and chanting Methi's name. To me, it sounded exactly the same as what my uncle had just been saying, but it was obviously quite different to their ears. One of them sprinted back to the village and returned after a couple of minutes with Methi. He was looking nervous. "You want me?" he asked. He must have thought we were accusing him of something. Had we returned to ask for our money back?

Uncle Harvey explained what he wanted.

Methi listened. Then nodded. For five thousand rupees, he would help us.

Uncle Harvey tried to bargain him down, but Methi refused to budge. Five thousand or nothing, he said.

Five thousand rupees is about one hundred dollars. That's a tidy sum of money at home, but a small fortune in India. Methi must have realized we were desperate. He knew he could ask for whatever he wanted. I started to feel angry with him, but then I remembered the rickety old shacks where these kids lived and decided they deserved all the money they could get from us.

Tanya had taken all the cash she could from an ATM and given it to us. Luckily we had enough. My uncle counted out three thousand rupees, pressed it into Methi's hand, and promised to pay the rest once we came out of the museum.

Now it was Methi's turn to argue and Uncle Harvey's not to budge. He wouldn't pay the full sum, he said, till he was sure Methi was telling the truth. Otherwise, said my uncle, Methi and his friends would take our money and give us nothing in return.

Methi talked to the other kids. They argued and waved

their arms. It looked as if they were about to break into a big fight. Methi kept gesturing in our direction. I hoped he was saying that we could be trusted. Eventually he and his friends said yes. Which was how the three of us came to be hiding behind one of the shacks at the edge of the village, listening for the sound of an engine.

# 41

**Methi heard it first.** He turned to us and put his finger to his lips.

We listened to the engine getting louder, coming closer. When it was almost level with our hiding place, a ball rolled through a gap between two huts and bounced into the road.

Two kids sprinted in hot pursuit. They appeared to be so focused on the ball that they hadn't even noticed the truck bearing down on them.

The driver slammed on his brakes.

The wheels screeched. The truck shuddered to a halt only a few inches from the boys. The driver leaned out of his window and yelled at them.

Their ball forgotten, they screamed back, shaking their fists. Who knows what they were saying, but it must have been rude enough to enrage the driver. His door swung open and he sprang out, determined to catch those pesky kids and show them who's boss.

I didn't see what happened next, because Methi had

pushed me into the road. Now I was scrambling into the back of the truck.

I rolled over, trying to keep out of sight, and came face-to-face with a goat.

It was lying on the floor of the truck, its front and back legs knotted together with brown twine. Its big black eyes stared at me in astonishment, then swiveled to look at my uncle rolling after me.

Poor old goat. Not only was it going to be eaten by tigers, but it had to spend the last few minutes of its life sharing its space with a pair of Trelawneys.

I squirmed against one wall of the truck, trying to keep out of the goat's way. Uncle Harvey pinned himself in the other corner. We'd barely taken our places when the truck jerked forward down the road. It drove a little way, then turned a corner and braked.

I heard voices. The driver was talking to the guards, probably complaining about the behavior of those kids. There was some loud laughter. Then we were moving again.

If the guards had looked into the back of the truck, they would have seen us immediately, but they didn't bother. The driver came here every day, bringing breakfast for the tigers, so they had no need to check on him.

Off we went again, through the gates, up the drive to the museum.

I wanted to sit up and wave to Methi, to say thank you, to promise to be back soon with the rest of his cash, but I knew I couldn't risk it. I didn't want to be seen. I tucked myself against the side of the truck and worried about what might happen next. I didn't want to feel scared. This was my plan. My idea. Uncle Harvey had agreed. Tanya had funded us. Methi had helped us. But the idea was mine. So was the responsibility. It had to work out. It had to.

The instant the truck stopped, my uncle rolled over the back. I scrambled after him. My eyes caught the goat's for an instant. Then I was landing on the earth with a jolt and running after my uncle.

# 42

**I had been worried** about guards and alarms, but there was no sign of either. The museum's front door was propped open with a broom, and the only sound in the air was birdsong.

My uncle leaped over the broom handle and ran inside. I was a couple of paces behind him.

The first gleams of the early-morning sunshine were shooting through the vast glass dome at the top of the museum. I could see a bucket and another broom, and two people, staring down at me. As we ran under them, Tipu Sultan and J.J. seemed to follow us with their eyes.

We sprinted up the main hallway. There were doors to the left, doors to the right, and a man up ahead.

A cleaner.

That wasn't in the plan.

He was holding a brush in one hand, a cloth in the other. He turned his head and stared dreamily at us, trying to make sense of the two people running toward him.

He opened his mouth and took a deep breath to scream for help.

Too late.

We were upon him. Not giving the cleaner time to make a noise, my uncle swung his fist and knocked him to the ground. Then he turned to me. "Sit on him!"

I did as I was told and sat on the poor guy, pinning him to the ground, my knee in the middle of his back. I'd done that before, but only to people I didn't like, such as bullies in the playground. Never to a complete stranger, and I didn't like doing it. The cleaner struggled, trying to turn himself around and tip me off. I pushed down on him with all my strength. He was bigger than me and I wouldn't have lasted long in a fair fight, but my uncle came to help just in time. He had pulled two cloths from the bucket. He tied one over the cleaner's mouth and used the other to tie his hands behind his back.

"Run," said my uncle.

"But shouldn't we—?"

He was already moving. I glanced once more at the cleaner, then sprinted after my uncle. The knots wouldn't hold for long: we'd just have to be quick.

We sprinted through the museum. I kept expecting to see another cleaner or a guard, but there was no one. Where were they? And why hadn't the alarms gone off yet? Where were the motion sensors, the laser beams, the sophisticated system that surely guarded J.J.'s priceless treasures? Had it been disabled so the cleaner could do his job?

Or were the alarms ringing right now in the nearest police station?

We had only been here once before, but the layout was very simple, so there was no chance of getting lost. Soon we arrived in the heart of the museum, that huge room with a throne standing in the center.

There it was. Tipu Sultan's throne. Covered in cushions and surrounded by the bejeweled heads of eight golden tigers, their rubies and emeralds glistening under the strong lights.

Eight tigers!

All of them were here. Ours and his.

What should we do? Take all eight? Or just nab ours and leave his?

Uncle Harvey pulled a black plastic bag from his pocket and reached for the nearest tiger. I didn't know if it was ours, and he obviously didn't care. He was just going to grab everything. Good decision, I thought. That way, J.J. would definitely have to deal with us. He might not hand over Marko in exchange for one tiger, but surely he'd surrender him for all eight.

Uncle Harvey's fingers encircled the tiger's neck. He lifted it up and turned to me, grinning with triumph. His mouth opened and he started to speak, but I never got to hear what he said, because at that moment the alarm went off.

It was the loudest noise I had ever heard. A scream that pierced my bones. I thought my ears were going to explode.

Uncle Harvey yelled something at me. I couldn't hear what he was saying, but I knew he was telling me to run.

He was already sprinting toward the exit.

I darted after him.

We hadn't even covered half the distance when a thick steel shutter slid smoothly down and covered the doorway.

I whirled around.

More steel shutters were sliding down over every door and window.

We were trapped.

# 43

**I ran one way** around the room and Uncle Harvey went the other, checking every door, searching for a crack or a crevice, some way to get out of here, but there was nothing. The steel shutters fitted the doors and windows perfectly, sealing this room like a fridge. Nothing could get in or out.

"Give me your phone," said my uncle.

I handed it over. He fiddled with the buttons, then shook his head.

"What's wrong?"

"I don't know. Either there's no reception or they've put something in here to block calls."

"So what are we going to do?"

"Sit and wait. There's nothing else we can do."

"We could fight our way out," I said.

"How?"

"With those." I pointed at the swords hanging from the walls.

We had no gunpowder or ammunition, so we couldn't use the muskets and pistols displayed in the glass cases at the end of the room, but the swords and spears displayed on the walls were in perfect working order, their blades so sharp and gleaming that they would have brought a satisfied smile to the lips of even the sternest sergeant inspecting his troops.

"Have you ever used a sword before?" asked Uncle Harvey.

"No. But I'm a fast learner."

"I guess it's better than nothing."

We chose our weapons. My uncle picked a British sword that would have belonged to an officer. Captain Hobson, perhaps, or even Horatio Trelawney himself. I found a smaller sword, a scimitar, which fit perfectly into my hand, and tucked a short dagger into the belt at the back of my trousers. The steel was icy against my skin.

"I like the feel of this," said my uncle, swinging his sword from side to side, its blade swishing through the air. "How's yours?"

"It's good."

There was a whirring sound and the steel shutters started rising, all of them moving at once. Sunlight flooded across the floor. I turned around, looking at door after door, searching for J.J. or the guards or the police. Which way would they come?

There. I could see feet. A pair of black shoes. Khaki trousers. A white shirt. And a face.

But it wasn't J.J.'s.

Marko smiled at us. Then he raised his right hand and

pointed a pistol at my uncle. "Put the swords on the floor," he said. "Do it very carefully, please. They're worth a lot of money."

"Where's J.J.?" asked my uncle.

"I don't know, mate, but I should think he's in bed."

"Does he know you're here?"

"Put the swords down," said Marko. "Then we'll talk."

I glanced at my uncle. He was placing his sword carefully, almost tenderly, on the floor. I did the same. We might have messed up our own lives, but there was no need to break these nice antiques. I wished I'd gotten a chance to fight with mine. I'd been looking forward to hacking my way out of here like a proper English gentleman.

"Thank you," said Marko. "Now come this way, please."

I said, "Where are you taking us?"

"You'll find out when we get there."

"Why are you here?" asked my uncle.

"I could be asking you the same question."

"You know why we're here. We want to get our tiger back. But why are you here?"

"If you really want to know, mate, I've been here all night. And all day yesterday. You've certainly taken your time, guys."

"How did you know we'd come here?" I said.

"It was pretty obvious," Marko said, glancing at me but keeping his attention mostly on my uncle. "I know what you guys are like. I've met three of you now and you're all the same. You don't think, do you? If you'd been thinking, you'd have got out of India as fast as you could and forgotten all about this dumb tiger. But you were too greedy, weren't you? Couldn't resist it. Had to come back and grab it. Just like I knew you would."

Marko was grinning, delighted by his own cleverness—and our stupidity. The terrible thing was, I couldn't disagree with him. We had been greedy and stupid. Just like he said, if we'd been sensible, if we'd thought things through properly, we would have fled. But I wanted to avenge Grandpa, and Uncle Harvey needed the cash, so we came back here. And the trap snapped shut around us.

We walked down the museum's long, elegant hallway. Marko ordered us to lead the way. He followed a few paces behind us, his gun trained on our backs. If we'd both started running in different directions at the same time, one of us might have been able to dodge through a door and get away, but the other would definitely have been shot dead. That was what I worked out, and my uncle must have come to the same decision, because neither of us tried anything. He did glance at me once. There was a strange expression in his eyes. I wasn't sure what it meant. But I smiled back, trying to look cheerful and positive, as if I was ready for whatever was going to happen next, and he gave me a wink. I think both of us knew we were in serious trouble.

The cleaner was still lying on the floor where we'd left him. But his head was in a pool of blood. He wasn't moving. Wasn't breathing. He was dead.

I stared at my uncle.

He said to Marko, "Why did you do that?"

"That wasn't me, mate. That was you."

"When I left him, he was alive."

"No one's going to believe that, are they?"

I said, "Why did you have to kill him? He didn't do anything to you! He was just a cleaner!"

"Some people are in the wrong place at the wrong time."

My uncle said, "Are you framing us for a murder?"

"That's enough talking," said Marko. We had reached the door at the end of the hallway. "Tom, you step outside first. Harvey, you follow him. No sudden movements, please. I don't want to have to shoot you."

We stepped over the broom and walked toward the wooden bridge.

Now I understood why Marko was alone. He didn't need anyone else to help him. And he didn't want any witnesses. He'd already tried to get us arrested for drug smuggling and put away, but that hadn't stopped us, so now he was going to frame us for murder. There was no one to stop him. He could do whatever he wanted with us. Only one person in the world knew we were here, and she was fast asleep in a hotel on the other side of town.

I felt horrible about the cleaner. Marko had murdered him, yes, but only to pin the blame on us, and so his death was really our responsibility. If we hadn't come here this morning, the cleaner would still be humming to himself as he mopped the floor and polished the white marble.

Marko walked us over the moat. I could see the three

tigers lying in the shade below us. A few bones lay in the dust, still covered with chunks of meat, the last remnants of that poor goat.

Ahead of us, down at the end of the driveway, I could see the gates and the guardhouse, but there was no sign of a car. What would Marko do? Deliver us to the guards and order them to call the police? Or was his car waiting on the other side of the gates? Or were reinforcements around the corner? Had he been lying about being here alone? Would J.J. step out and confront us?

"Stop," said Marko.

We were halfway across the wooden bridge.

"Turn round."

We turned to face him. The sun was shining in my eyes and I could hear birds chirping in the trees. If things had been different, it would have been a beautiful day.

Marko was about two yards from us. I stared into the eye of his gun. It was pointed more at my uncle than me, which I suppose was sensible, although I couldn't help feeling a bit insulted. Wasn't he worried about me? Didn't he think I might try to hurt him?

"You can choose who goes first," said Marko.

It took me a moment to understand what he meant.

"Let him go," said my uncle, who had understood immediately. Maybe he'd already guessed what was going to happen and had been waiting for this moment. "He's just a kid. He won't say anything about what you've done. Even if he does, no one will believe him."

"I wish that were true," replied Marko. "But even kids get listened to. Sorry, guys. I like you both. If things were different, we might have been friends. But like I said, you can choose who jumps first. Or you can both go down there together and take your chances with the tigers. You never know, maybe you can fight them off. Two against three—the odds aren't bad. However you go, you're going to have to choose soon." He waggled the gun at us. "Come on, make your minds up. Who's first?"

"Me," I said, taking a step forward.

"No." My uncle took a step himself. "It's me."

"I don't care which it is," said Marko. "But don't come any closer."

"You can't do this," said my uncle. "You'll never get away with it."

"Of course I will. Two burglars break into the museum, kill a cleaner, then panic, run away and miss their footing. One of them fell down first and the other tried to rescue him. No one's going to question it. Go on, then. Get down there, Tom. Take your chances with the tiger."

"He's not going anywhere," said my uncle. "Nor am I."

"Don't make me shoot you," said Marko.

"If you want to kill me, you're going to have to kill me like a man. You're going to have to look into my eyes and shoot me."

"You'd rather be shot than take your chances with a tiger?"

"Yes."

"Fine. Then I'll shoot you." Marko pointed the pistol at the center of my uncle's chest. I could see his finger tightening on the trigger.

"Wait!" I said.

It was just enough to distract Marko. He turned his head to glance at me, but I'd already moved. I swung my arm behind my back, yanked out the dagger that had been tucked into my belt, and threw it at him.

I'm not great at throwing knives, but I'm not bad, either. I spent one summer practicing with my friend Finn. We found an old door abandoned in a field, tipped it on its side, and propped it against a couple of crates and stole a knife from each of our kitchens. Day after day, we threw our knives against the door. *Thwack. Thwack. Thwack.* For hours and hours. *Thwack. Thwack. Thwack.* By the end of the summer, we promised ourselves, one of us would be able to stand against the door and the other would throw knives around him, missing every time, just like in a circus.

We were never actually that good. But I was accurate enough to hit Marko.

Not where I wanted to, unfortunately. I'd been aiming for his heart and I got his ankle. But it was still enough to knock him off balance for a moment, which gave me and my uncle time to run the short distance dividing us from him.

I heard a shot. I didn't know where it went. Then we crashed into Marko.

He fell backwards.

I felt his hand clawing at my face, yanking my hair.

He was toppling over the balcony.

Falling from the bridge.

Rolling down the slope.

He landed at the bottom with a thud.

The tigers had seen him coming. They were already on their feet. They looked graceful, even lazy, but they moved very fast, springing out of the shade and across their enclosure.

Marko didn't waste a moment checking his wounds or looking at us. He knew survival was all that mattered. He pushed himself into a shooting position, one knee on the ground, the other leg bent, his gun raised and held with both hands, giving him a steady aim.

He pulled the trigger. There was a loud bang and the biggest of the tigers winced and roared and rolled to the ground, its legs thrashing. I could see blood pumping across its sleek fur and spitting into the dust.

Marko was already turning to point his gun at the next of them, but the tigers were almost on him. He fired. Another bang. The second tiger roared in fury and pain, but Marko's aim hadn't been so good this time, and his shot had only wounded it, enraging it further, making it more determined.

He managed to fire three more shots, but the tigers had reached him by now, and the bullets went wide.

It was over very quickly. Marko made a terrible sound, halfway between a scream and a gurgle, then he was quiet.

Uncle Harvey was already walking toward the exit. I ran after him. "Have you still got it?"

He didn't have to ask what I was talking about. He just patted his pocket. "Right here."

The three of us ran down the driveway to the big steel gate: me, my uncle, and Tipu's tiger. We didn't know if it was the right one, but it didn't really matter. All eight were more or less the same. At least we had one of them.

As we approached the guardroom, we heard voices. A man and a woman were shouting at each other in an Indian language. I glanced at my uncle. He shrugged his shoulders. We walked nearer. A third voice joined the other two, another man, speaking slowly and persuasively. The guardroom door was open. We looked inside. Screens showed what was happening in and around the museum, displaying footage from the different rooms, the entrances and exits. The voices came from a small TV. A man was sprawled on the floor. The side of his head was matted with hair and blood. Marko must have killed him, too. Maybe they had sat here together, watching our progress on the cameras, while Marko waited for the perfect moment to come and confront us.

"We should call the police," I said.

"We will. Later." My uncle stepped carefully into the room, pacing around the guard's corpse, and looked at the control panel by the door. He tried four buttons before finding the right one. Then the big steel gate swung open.

# 44

***Methi walked us to a taxi.*** We paid him the rest of his money, said goodbye, and headed into the center of town. Uncle Harvey called the police and suggested they pay a visit to J.J.'s museum. He kept the call short and didn't give his own name. He switched off the phone and turned to me. "Ready for breakfast?"

"What about the tiger?"

"What about it?"

"What are we going to do with it?"

"Sell it to J.J. for two million dollars."

"I've got a better idea."

"Oh, yeah? What's that?"

I told him.

Uncle Harvey listened in silence. Then he sighed. "I suppose that would be the right thing to do. But what about me? What about my debts?"

"You said you'd find some way to pay them."

"I suppose I will. Fine, let's do the right thing. I might as well act like a nice guy for once in my life."

When we got to the hotel, Tanya was still asleep, but she woke up as soon as we walked through the door. I stared out of the window while she got dressed and Uncle Harvey told her what had happened. We paid the bill and took another taxi to the train station. Wherever we went, I was expecting to be surrounded by armed police and arrested, but no one took any notice of us, or no more than usual, anyway. Beggars asked for money and kids tried to persuade us to buy tea or sweets, but no one demanded to see our passports or asked what we knew about a dead cleaner and a mauled Australian. Where was J.J.? And his SWAT team? What were they waiting for? Why weren't they grabbing the tiger back from us? Maybe he didn't really have all the information in the world at his fingertips. Maybe he hadn't tracked us with CCTVs and satellites. Maybe we'd escaped.

We called Suresh from the train and asked him to meet us at the station. When we strolled down the platform, he was waiting for us. He stared in astonishment at our bruised faces. "Who has done this to you?"

"We were robbed," said my uncle.

"Who did rob you?" He sound personally affronted, as if he wanted to track down the robbers and exact vengeance on our behalf.

"It's a long story," said Uncle Harvey.

"I will take you to a doctor. There is a good one in Mysore. It is not far from here."

"We don't need a doctor. We want to go back to the temple."

"Ah, the temple. There is terrible problems at the temple."

Suresh told us everything on the drive north, shouting over his shoulder, describing the fire and its after-effects. A wall had collapsed and broken a man's leg. The temple would have to be rebuilt, but the priests had no money. They didn't know what to do. They had asked all the local villagers to contribute, but none of them had anything to spare.

"Something will turn up," said my uncle.

"I hope so." Suresh flashed a grin back at us, then returned his attention to the road.

I wanted to know more about the man who had broken his leg. That was my fault. Would he be able to walk again? Suresh said yes, he was going to be fine, he would just have to spend a few months on crutches. I still felt terrible. I remembered the guard and the cleaner in J.J.'s museum, those two men who had lost their lives because of me, and I wished I'd never come to India. Then I thought about my grandfather and remembered that I would never get to see him again, never go walking with him over the Irish hills or sit at his kitchen table, hearing his stories about his crazy life, and I understood that Marko was the person who was really responsible for all this carnage. If he'd just made a deal with Grandpa, J.J. would have the letters and the tiger safely in his museum and the cleaner and the guard would still be alive, and so would my grandfather.

When we arrived at the village, all four of us climbed to the summit together. As we came closer, I saw the first evidence of fire damage. A tree had lost its leaves. The branches were blackened and bare. Straw roofs had been reduced to a few twisted rafters. Statues were smothered in soot. I had never meant for all this to happen.

We took off our shoes and left them on the racks. I was amazed to see my sneakers were still there. No one had touched them.

Suresh led us through the courtyards to the inner sanctum.

The elephant was still tied up and had the same glum expression on his face, but he looked unhurt.

The man on one leg was in his place, standing on the same leg. Had he stayed like that while the flames raged around him?

In the inner sanctum, three pilgrims were sitting cross-legged on the floor, their hands folded in front of their chests. Two women were placing offerings of food in little wooden bowls. A bare-chested man was lighting candles. He had his back to us, but when he turned around, I saw that he was Ram. He blinked at us, as if he thought he ought to know who we were but couldn't quite place us. Then he saw Suresh and remembered everything. He came over, grinning joyfully. "Hello. You have come back to see our temple again? Welcome."

I glanced at my uncle. He nodded. We hadn't rehearsed what to say, or who would say it, but I knew it should be me who talked. I stepped forward and said, "We want to give you something."

# 45

**At *six o'clock that evening,*** J.J. marched into the inner sanctum accompanied by Vivek, Meera, and three other advisors. They were in their usual uniforms: jeans and a T-shirt for him, designer suits for the others. Earlier in the day, Uncle Harvey had called J.J. and asked him to come and meet us. J.J. argued a bit, threatening to call the police, but Uncle Harvey advised him not to bother. If he wanted his tiger, my uncle said, he should come straight here and talk to us. So J.J. did. He arrived in one of his helicopters, landing in the village and jogging up the hill to the temple. I didn't see him myself—I was waiting in the inner sanctum—but I heard later that he'd run up the stairs two at a time and arrived at the top not even out of breath. Suresh and Ram had been there to meet him. They led him into a room in the temple, where we were waiting with some of the priests.

Ignoring everyone else, J.J. marched straight up to my uncle and held out his hand. "My tiger, please."

"We have to talk first," said Uncle Harvey.

"It is here?"

"Yes."

"Where? I want to see it."

"You'll see it soon enough. First we have to talk."

"If you want to talk, you can talk with my lawyers. They say you don't have a case. You are a dealer in stolen property. The tiger is not yours."

"I know it's not."

"You know?"

"Yes. My ancestor stole it. I don't have any rights over it. I know that."

"Then give it to me."

"It's not yours, either. It's theirs." Uncle Harvey pointed at Ram and the other priests.

They were wearing plastic flip-flops and white sheets wrapped around their waists. J.J. and his advisors had phones and computers and a helicopter waiting outside. If I had been Ram or another of the priests, I would have felt intimidated, if not actually terrified, to be confronted by this slick parade of money and power, but they didn't seem bothered, just smiling and nodding, confirming that the tiger was theirs. "This is correct," said Ram, speaking for all of them. "The tiger is ours. It has resided in this temple for many years, bringing good fortune to our people."

J.J. didn't argue about ownership. His lawyers must have advised him already that a judge would rule in the temple's favor. He simply said, "I want to buy it."

"That is not possible, sir."

"Name your price."

"I am sorry, sir. The tiger belongs in our temple. It is not for sale."

"I will give you two million dollars," said J.J. "U.S. dollars. American dollars. Will that satisfy you?"

Ram smiled. "I am sorry."

"That's not enough?"

"We do not wish to sell."

"How about two and a half million!"

"No, sir."

"You don't want two and a half million dollars?"

"No, sir."

"You drive a hard bargain, my friend. You're a good negotiator. But I want this tiger and I'm willing to pay for it. If you let me take the tiger away today, I will give you three million dollars."

Ram appeared to believe this whole thing was a joke. He was smiling broadly, shaking his head, refusing to be bought. "Thank you, sir, but I will not take your money."

"You understand how much that is?" J.J. turned to his entourage. "Meera, what's three million dollars in rupees?"

Her face scrunched up in concentration. "Three million dollars is—"

"Excuse me for interrupting," said Ram. "But there is no need to make a calculation. I understand what is a dollar. I know what is three million. The answer is no. The tiger will be staying here."

"You're refusing three million dollars?"

"Yes, sir."

"How about four million?"

"This tiger is not for sale, sir."

"Are you serious? You won't sell it for four million dollars?"

"No, sir."

"Four. Million. Dollars. Do you know what that means?"

"Yes, sir."

"You don't. You've never seen the power of money like that. I have. I can tell you, it means everything." J.J. shook his head and smiled ruefully. "Do you know how much this tiger is actually worth? Two million at the most. Probably one and a half on the open market. You're never going to be made an offer like this again. Take the cash!"

"No, sir," said Ram.

"Why not?"

"Because the tiger is not for sale."

J.J. still wasn't ready to give up. He glanced around the chamber as if he was checking who could hear him, then very slowly said, "I want this tiger and I am willing to pay for it. I will give you five million dollars."

Meera put her hand on J.J.'s arm, but he pushed her away. All his attention was focused on the priest, waiting for an answer.

Ram said, "Five million dollars U.S.?"

"Yes."

"How much this is in rupees?"

Meera told him.

Ram smiled at J.J. "Yes, sir."

J.J. gave my uncle a fierce grin of triumph. Then he was hidden behind Meera and Vivek and his other advisors, who crowded around him, slapping him on the back and taking turns to shake his hand as if he was a boxer who'd just won the biggest fight of his life.

# 46

***J.J. arranged for us*** to be provided with new passports. He could afford to be generous. He'd got what he wanted. He'd had to pay for it, of course, but we soon understood that the whole thing had been a coordinated PR stunt, designed to wash away the blood spilled at his museum. Giving five million dollars to a temple, paying for repairs and renovations, made him look like a good Hindu and a true Indian patriot. That's what the papers said. The headlines proclaimed him a saint. No one was rude enough to mention the deaths of a cleaner, a guard, or an Australian mercenary.

J.J. settled things with the police, too. He even offered to pay us ten thousand dollars for Horatio Trelawney's letters. They would be housed in the museum's archives, he said, and made available to historians who wished to research the life and times of Tipu Sultan.

Uncle Harvey negotiated the price up to fifty thousand, then said yes. The money would cover our tickets and help to pay off a few of his most dangerous debts. He'd missed out on five million dollars, but at least his legs were safe.

J.J. swore that he had known nothing about my grandfather. He admitted that Marko had been his employee, but claimed to have no control over the Australian. I didn't believe him, but my uncle told me not to worry about it. There was nothing we could do, he said. His father, my grandfather, was dead, and the man who killed him was dead too, and that was the end of that.

We stayed two more nights in Srirangapatna after J.J. had gone. I had my own room in the hotel and my own cash to spend on whatever I wanted. "Here's your pocket money," said Uncle Harvey, handing over a thick bundle of bills. I thought I was rich till I translated them into dollars and realized he'd only given me about twenty bucks.

"Where's my half?" I said.

"Which half?"

"We agreed to split all the money fifty-fifty, remember? You owe me twenty-five thousand."

"I could give you that money, Tom. But then I wouldn't be able to pay off my debts, and both my legs would get broken. Is that what you want? If it is, I'll give you the money. Say the word. The choice is yours."

I sighed. "Keep it."

"Thank you."

After that, I didn't see much more of my uncle. He disappeared with Tanya. We did run into each other once in the hotel lobby, and he apologized for deserting me. "I'm sorry, but I can't help myself. I've got to be with her. I think I'm falling in love."

"Don't worry," I said. "I'm having fun too."

And I was. I liked having the freedom of the city. I spent all my time wandering through the streets, seeing the sights of Srirangapatna, doing the full Tipu tour. I hadn't realized that the town was an island sitting in the middle of a river, which was what made it such a good fortress. I walked along the remains of the walls, imagining Horatio scrambling over them, dodging cannonballs, ducking under swishing scimitars, searching for the sultan and his treasure.

I spent most of my time with Suresh. When we weren't walking around the city, he let me drive his rickshaw. It was fantastic. It didn't go very fast, but we chug-chug-chugged out of Srirangapatna and down a main road, puttering through the traffic, the wind whistling in our hair. We even picked up a passenger, a woman with six shopping bags. She paid us twenty rupees to take her home and gave me two extra as a tip.

That same day, Suresh took me to his house, where I met his mom, his brother, and his sisters. They lived together in two tiny rooms, one for eating and the other for sleeping, the six of them sharing a big mattress spread out on the floor.

When I arrived, Suresh's mom was sitting in a wicker chair in the corner of the room, and she never moved from there. Her face was gaunt and I could see that every breath was an effort. But she smiled joyfully when she met me, and took my hand in both of hers, and talked to me via Suresh, with him translating whatever she wanted to say. She was pleased to meet me, she said, and pleased I was friends with her son, and thanked me over and over again for the money that we'd given her.

I said it wasn't really my money; it was the temple's. Once the repairs had been paid for, the rest would be used to build a medical center in Srirangapatna and pack it with all the most up-to-date medical equipment.

On the third day, Suresh drove all three of us to the station in his rickshaw, and we said goodbye. He said he'd email me with news about his mom. I promised to send him a Red Sox shirt as soon as I got back to the U.S.

I didn't know how, when, or where, but I was sure I'd see him again one day, and I think he felt the same way.

We said goodbye to Tanya there too. She was catching a train to Mysore and then heading to Mumbai for the last few days of her vacation. Our train left an hour later than hers, going the other way, taking us to Bangalore. From the station, we would catch a taxi to the airport and take a plane home.

Kids hurried along the platform, shouting "Chai! Chai!" I remembered the boy in Bangalore whose chai I'd stolen and hoped I'd see him there again. I wanted to pay him for a full pot.

Tanya gave me a big hug and said she was very happy to have met me. Then she and Uncle Harvey kissed for a long time. They probably would have carried on all day, but a guard blew his whistle and waved a green flag. The train was about to leave. Tanya clambered aboard, swung her backpack into a luggage rack, and leaned out the window, waving and blowing kisses.

"See you in Tel Aviv," she shouted as the train pulled out of the station.

My uncle kept on waving till she was out of sight, then turned to me. "When does our train leave?"

"Not for another hour."

"How about a coffee?"

"I wouldn't mind a mango lassi."

The station café was crowded, but we found some space at the bar. We sat on tall stools and leaned our elbows on the counter. On the wall above us there was a huge poster of the Taj Mahal. The waiter wore black trousers and a spotless white shirt. He nodded as he hurried past and promised to take our order as soon as he could.

I asked Uncle Harvey when he was planning to visit Tel Aviv.

"Oh, I don't know. One of these days."

"I thought you'd fallen in love."

"I have. But that doesn't mean I have to go to Tel Aviv."

"I thought you were about to marry her."

"Marry her? Why would I want to do that?"

"I don't know. You seem to like her so much."

"I do like her, but that doesn't mean I have to marry her. I'm too young to settle down."

I thought of my dad, who was only two years and five months older than Uncle Harvey but had settled down a gazillion years ago, marrying Mom, having Grace, then me and then Jack, giving himself up to a life of mortgages and retirement funds and working five days a week and washing his car on the weekends.

Could Uncle Harvey ever be like that?

Could he ever have a wife and kids and an ordinary life?

I hoped not.

# 47

**We flew back to JFK,** then caught a cab into New York to pick up Uncle Harvey's car. He insisted on driving me home. I said I was happy to take the bus, but he wouldn't let me.

He has a nice car, a silver Mercedes with black leather seats, and the ride was so smooth that I fell asleep right away. When I woke up, we were almost home.

The streets of Norwich looked more familiar than my own face. That might sound poetic, but it's actually true. I had caught sight of myself in the mirror in the bathroom on the plane and seen someone I didn't recognize. Who was that guy? Where had he been? He looked rough. There was a purplish bruise around his right eye, his skin was raw and peeling from several days of sunburn, and half-healed scabs speckled his cheeks and forehead.

We parked outside my house and walked up the front path together. I rang the doorbell. I knew they'd be home, because we'd already called them to say roughly what time we'd be arriving.

There was a short pause. Just long enough for me and Uncle Harvey to exchange a quick smile.

Then the door opened.

Mom took one look at my bruises and wrapped me in her arms.

I emerged from her embrace to find Dad fixing me with a stern look.

"You're grounded," he said. "Forever."

"What do you mean?"

"I mean you're grounded until the end of time. Or the day you leave home. Whichever comes first."

"You can't do that."

"I can do what I want. I'm your father."

"You can't actually prevent me from leaving the house."

"I can. And I will. Maybe next time you'll think twice before hopping onto a plane with your uncle and running off to some foreign country."

"Try to stop me."

"That's exactly what I'm going to do."

We stared at each other like two Mafia bosses negotiating over a slice of the city. Then Dad said, "Go to your room."

"The thing is—" I started to say, but he interrupted before I got any further.

"I don't want to hear your excuses."

"I wasn't going to make any excuses."

"Yes, you were."

"I wasn't, actually. I was going to tell you about finding the guy who murdered your father."

"I don't want to hear about it. Go to your room."

"Don't you want to know what happened?"

"Not now, no. Go to your room."

"I will. When I've said goodbye to Uncle Harvey."

"Fine. Do it. Be quick."

I turned to my uncle. "Bye."

"Bye, Tom. Look after yourself."

"I will."

"Right," said Dad. "You've said goodbye. Now go to your room." He turned to my uncle. "I think you'd better leave, Harvey."

"You're not going to invite me in for a drink?"

"No."

"Not even a cup of tea?"

"No."

"Can I use your loo? I've got a long drive home."

"There's a pub round the corner. You can go there."

"Fine." Uncle Harvey paused for a moment as if he was thinking of the right words to use, but he must have decided it was better to say nothing at all, because he just said, "Bye, guys."

I got one last glimpse of him walking down the path toward his car, then Dad closed the front door and sent me to my room.

I thought Jack and Grace might be lying in wait to hear all about my adventures, but they were nowhere to be seen. Maybe they'd been warned not to talk to me. I had bought them both great presents from India: a carved wooden elephant for him, a bundle of spices for her, cardamon pods and cinnamon sticks and fennel seeds and many more, each in its own little muslin bag.

I dumped my bag on the floor and stretched out on my bed. After several nights of cheap hotels, followed by a night on a plane, my own mattress felt beautiful. But I couldn't sleep. I was wide awake. Thoughts buzzed through my skull. I lay there, staring at the posters on the walls, the cracks on the ceiling, all the things that I knew so well, and remembered what Dad had said.

Could he actually ground me forever?

Would he really be able to stop me leaving the house?

No way.

I rolled off my bed and walked to the window.

Through the glass, I could see the same view I'd seen every morning I could remember. Our car was parked outside the house, but there was no sign of Uncle Harvey's. He had already left.

I undid the latch and opened the window. The breeze felt cold. I still hadn't adjusted to the change in temperature.

My room was on the second floor, but there was a sloping roof directly under me.

I climbed out the window, scrambled down the roof, and dangled my legs off the edge. If anyone had been looking out the front window, they would have seen my shoes. Best not to hang around. I pushed myself off.

The ground came to meet me with a bump.

I sprang up, dusted the gravel off my hands, and started walking quickly down the street.